BRIDES OF WILDCAT COUNTY

IMPETUOUS: MATTIE'S STORY

D1550972

BRIDES OF WILDCAT COUNTY

IMPETUOUS: MATTIE'S STORY

JUDE WATSON

Aladdin Paperbacks

First Aladdin Paperbacks edition January 1996

Copyright © 1996 by Jude Watson

Aladdin Paperbacks
An imprint of Simon & Schuster
Children's Publishing Division
1230 Avenue of the Americas
New York, NY 10020

Designed by Randall Sauchuck

Printed and bound in the United States of America

10 9 8 7 6 5 4 3 2 1

Library of Congress Cataloging-in-Publication Data
Watson, Jude.
Impetuous : Mattie's story / Jude Watson. — 1st Aladdin Paperbacks ed.
p. cm. — (Brides of Wildcat County)
Summary: Seventeen-year-old Mattie leaves her sister Ivy in Last Chance,
California, and disguises herself as a boy in order to get a job with the Pony
Express, finding adventure, facing danger, and falling in love.
ISBN 0-689-80329-X
[1. Frontier and pioneer life—West (U.S.)—Fiction.
2. Pony Express—Fiction. 3. Sex role—Fiction. 4. West (U.S.)—Fiction.]
I. Title. II. Series: Watson, Jude. Brides of Wildcat County.
PZ7.W32755Im 1996
[Fic]—dc20 95-35907

BRIDES OF WILDCAT COUNTY

IMPETUOUS: MATTIE'S STORY

CHAPTER ONE
TEN THOUSAND WAYS TO SAY NO

"Mattie, you can't!"

Mattie Nesbitt had been hearing those words all her life. Back in Maine, after she'd climbed the fence in the garden when she was seven. When she'd worn trousers underneath her skirt at ten. When she'd sailed alone on the bay at fourteen and had been foolish enough to confess it.

The loudest "you can't" had been shrilled by her Aunt Pru when Mattie had told her she was moving to California. At sixteen Mattie had packed up her sister and herself and had headed west.

There were probably ten thousand ways to say no, and she'd heard them all.

"It's improper. It just isn't done. You'll disgrace the family. No one will marry you. . . ."

Today it was a bit more commonplace.

"You'll never get a dancing partner in that!" her

sister Ivy exclaimed. Her usually mild expression was horrified.

Mattie looked down at the boy's pants she bought at the miner's supply shop in town. "But I shined my boots," she told Ivy, sticking out one foot to demonstrate. She saw a clot of mud on the side and quickly tucked it back before Ivy's sharp eyes could catch it. "And I'm wearing a white shirt," she added. Usually she was partial to the same red or blue flannel as the miners wore.

Ivy crossed her arms.

"Besides," Mattie said, "I don't *want* to dance."

"Of course you want to dance," Ivy said, her amber eyes amused. "You can't fool me. Now, where is your blue calico? I bought that material from Opal especially for you. It matches your eyes perfectly."

Ivy held up the cornflower blue gown with its yellow sash. It was the prettiest dress Mattie had ever owned, and today was the perfect day to wear it. The two sisters were attending a three-county celebration in the neighboring town of Grass Valley. There would be prizes for food and crafts, a horse race, and, most interesting to the girls of Last Chance, a dance.

Ivy shook out the blue dress. "There. And I have

a pretty blue ribbon for your hair. Do you want to wear my cameo?"

"I'd just lose it, most likely," Mattie said grumpily, throwing herself down to sprawl in a chair.

Ivy winced, but she didn't correct Mattie's unlady-like posture. She knew she'd have a hard enough time getting Mattie into the dress.

"Now, where are your good boots?" she asked, looking under Mattie's bed. Mattie and Ivy shared the long, low-ceilinged room with four other girls who had come with them to find husbands in California. Next door, six other girls shared similar room.

All the girls had set sail from New York together. They had all read Elijah Bullock's "Brides Wanted" newspaper advertisement and, for varying reasons, determined to go.

It had been nine months since their arrival. The Bullock family was no longer paying their board. Two girls were married and three more were engaged, but there were still ten unattached "brides" living in Annie Friend's boardinghouse. Narcissa Pratt blamed Ivy for the rest of them not having suitors because she was waiting to marry her beau Justus Calhoun.

If Narcissa was bitter, Mattie was delighted to still

be free. Back in Maine, she'd thought in her practical way that she'd be married within six months of arriving in California. To her mind, one man was as good as another, as long as he was presentable and earned a good wage.

But after a few months in the Sierra, Mattie had been less interested in the young men who came calling than in the possibilities around her. She had discovered that hauling freight and letters around the mining towns could make her a good living. She'd scraped together a bit of money and bought a horse and wagon.

She didn't need a man the way she had back east. There was no one looking over her shoulder, wagging a finger at the sight of a young woman working. Plenty of females worked in California. They ran boardinghouses and laundries and restaurants—she'd even heard about a lady doctor up in Oregon!

Some of her fellow brides also earned their own living. Ivy was a successful author. Fanny Mulrooney took in washing. Opal Pollard had left the boardinghouse and opened up her own dressmaking business. Malinda Burden was a waitress at the Golden Spur Restaurant in town, and Dottie Barbee and Georgina Temple had their own pie-making business.

They were all finding their way. Which was precisely why Mattie wanted to wear her work clothes to Grass Valley.

"I thought I could pick up a job there," Mattie told Ivy as her sister smoothed out a length of blue ribbon. "I hate to travel all that way to a town and not make a profit, Ivy. And I haven't cracked those northern mining towns yet. There's lots of business there, I'll warrant—"

"You can take a day off," Ivy said. "Now get dressed proper. Justus will be here any minute to pick us up."

"I thought I'd take my wagon—"

"You're coming with us in the buggy," Ivy said in a tone that brooked no argument. She strode out of the room, her skirt swishing around her ankles. "And don't forget your bonnet and gloves!" she flung over her shoulder.

Mattie sighed. Her sweet-tempered, shy sister had certainly changed over the past nine months. Living in the mountains had snapped some steel into her spine. And becoming a newspaperwoman had made her positively bossy. Even though at seventeen Mattie was a year younger than Ivy, she'd usually been the one to make decisions. In Mattie's opinion, Ivy was reasserting her position as head of the family a little too firmly.

Still, she rarely chose to cross her older sister. Mattie slipped the dress over her head and tied the yellow sash. It was a becoming dress, she had to admit. And she supposed that tying her hair with a blue ribbon was prettier than scraping it back with a leather thong.

But she still didn't look like a lady, Mattie thought with a sigh as she squinted into the small mirror over the dresser. Her auburn hair was too unruly, and she was freckled from spending so much time outdoors. And somehow, riding astride a horse was causing her to walk in a most unladylike manner. She had a tendency to stride, and Ivy was always telling her to slow down.

Down below, she heard the sound of a horse and buggy. Mattie peeked out the window and saw Justus pull up in front of the boardinghouse. He climbed down, the sun glinting on his blond hair. A wide smile creased his face as Ivy walked out to greet him.

A pang of envy pierced Mattie's heart. How nice it must be for Ivy to see a face light up just for her! The couple had had their share of trouble finding each other, but everyone knew it was only a matter of time before they were married. Despite Narcissa's impatience—actually, Mattie suspected that

Narcissa only wanted a share of Ivy's dresser drawers—Ivy had put off her marriage. She wanted their lives to be a little more settled first.

Lately the trouble between the States was weighing on everyone's mind. Justus was from Georgia, and his father was already pressuring him to return and join the militia. Justus wouldn't go back, but he was afraid to break with his father. He'd often said the "peculiar institution" of slavery was a shame upon the soul of their nation.

Mattie thought Justus had a tendency to brood. She wouldn't like that in a man. Why didn't he just tell his father to go hang?

All this war talk was foolish, anyway. In this peaceful summer of 1860, war seemed impossible to Mattie. The nation was growing by leaps and bounds. Oregon had entered the Union a year ago. Settlers were pouring into Nevada and Utah. There was now regular stagecoach service back east. Why would a nation just beginning to grow split apart? It didn't make sense to Mattie, and privately, she felt the long, serious talks Ivy had with Justus were pure bunkum.

Mattie snatched up her bonnet with a sigh. With all of her envy at Ivy's happiness, she wouldn't change places with her. Having a beau involved too much worry. It was downright tedious having to fret about someone else all the time.

"Are you ready, Mattie?" Ivy called upstairs. Mattie hurried out to the head of the stairs, and Ivy beamed approvingly at her. "How nice you look."

"That's a very pretty dress, Mattie," Justus said.

Mattie did an exaggerated curtsey that ended in a pratfall. She stuck her feet out from under her dress and grinned as Justus burst out laughing.

"Justus, you *do* encourage her," Ivy said mildly. "How am I to turn this ruffian into a lady with you thwarting me at every turn?" But Mattie heard the amusement in Ivy's voice. She knew Ivy was fighting her own impulse to laugh.

Justus slid an arm around Ivy's waist. "Mattie's got something better than airs and graces, love," he said.

"Guts," Mattie said, bouncing to her feet and starting down the stairs.

Ivy shuddered. "Mattie, must you use that horrid word?"

"I was going to say courage," Justus said lightly.

"Courage won't get her a beau," Ivy said decidedly, wrapping her light shawl around her shoulders. "Grace will."

"Who's Grace?" Mattie asked innocently. Justus smiled, then assumed a poker face for Ivy's sake.

Ivy giggled. She could never retain her severity for long. "Come along, you two," she said with mock sternness. "It is perfectly clear that I will be acting as chaperon today."

Mattie hesitated. "I forgot something in my room. I'll be right there."

Quickly, she raced back up the stairs. In the bedroom, she bundled up her boots, pants, and man's white shirt. Then she grabbed her broad-brimmed hat and hurried back downstairs. Justus and Ivy were still in the parlor, and she slipped out the front door to the buggy.

She shoved her bundle way underneath the backseat. If she managed to get a job in Grass Valley, she could always borrow a horse from a buddy. She could tell Ivy that she was getting a ride home from someone else, then make a freight run.

Ivy and Justus emerged from the boardinghouse just as she shoved her heavy boots out of sight.

"What in tarnation has been keeping you two?" she complained amiably. "Are you figuring on getting to Grass Valley the middle of next week?"

"That's enough out of you," Justus said with a wink as he helped Ivy into the buggy.

Mattie settled back in her seat. She might be wearing a dress and ribbons, but she could turn herself into a freight hauler in a twinkling. One result of having so much experience with *no* was that sooner or later, you learned how to weasel your way around it.

CHAPTER TWO
THE STRANGER

The streets of Grass Valley were thronged with people. Justus's buggy slowed to a crawl as they made their way to the fairgrounds on the edge of town. The planked sidewalks were too narrow to hold the crowd, and folks spilled out into the street. Ladies in light summer dresses swung their parasols, chattering to their companions. The men all looked freshly shaved and proud of it. They were dressed in their Sunday suits and best hats.

They left the horse and buggy in the care of a man in a pasture adjoining the fairgrounds. They joined the milling crowd as they ambled past booths offering pies, refreshments, jams, jellies, and quilts. It seemed as though the entire population of the Sierra was there to celebrate the arrival of warm weather at last.

Around her, Mattie heard the sound of the unfamiliar Cornish accents of the area's newest settlers.

She heard rough miner talk, cultivated ladies oohing over the wares, and children laughing. It was strange not to hear the noise of the massive mills that powered the vast mines outside of town. Today everyone had the day off.

They followed the sound of a fiddle toward the dance floor. Ivy's foot tapped as they stopped at the edge of the wooden platform constructed just for the occasion.

"Doesn't it make you want to dance, Mattie?"

"No," Mattie said shortly.

Snowy mountain passes didn't scare her. Treacherous muddy roads didn't slow her down. But dancing—that was enough to chill her blood.

It wasn't that she *couldn't* dance. It was that she got so all-fired nervous when she *did*. But she never admitted to anyone when she was afraid— not even Ivy.

"I don't know, Ivy," Mattie drawled as they watched the dancers. "You can call it dancing. But being grappled by a dusty miner isn't tempting in the least."

"Oh, don't be so particular, Mattie," Ivy said, sliding her arm in her sister's. She pressed it. "Isn't there one young man here you'd dance with? They aren't *all* dusty miners. Isn't there even one person you might fancy? Just for the few minutes on the dance floor, that is."

Just to be polite, Mattie gave a perfunctory glance over the crowd. She was already shaking her head when a young man caught her eye. She stopped shaking her head and stared.

He was a stranger. She couldn't say what about him had caused her to stop and examine him more closely. It wasn't that he was taller than anyone else. As a matter of fact, he was only an inch or two taller than she was. It wasn't that he was handsomer than the other fellows or cleaner or better dressed. He wore the same white shirt, dark pants, and suspenders that most of the young men wore.

It was the way he stood, Mattie decided. Some quality of watchfulness, of quiet, was present in every line of his body. He wasn't grinning like the other men or clapping his hands or, worst of all, pretending he didn't care about the swirling dresses and the tossing curls of the pretty girls.

His grave face took it all in without judgment. She couldn't tell the color of his eyes, but she knew their expression would be as watchful and still as his wiry body was. His black hair was long, falling to his shoulders, and he was clean shaven. Most of the men in the Sierra wore beards. His complexion was dark, as though he spent time outdoors.

"That one?" Ivy asked.

Mattie blushed, realizing that her sister had followed her gaze. She must be staring like a dumbstruck cow.

"The rough-looking one with the long hair?" Ivy asked doubtfully. "Well, there *is* something about him, I declare—"

Mattie's auburn curls flew as she looked away. "Please, Ivy," she whispered, her face hot. "Stop looking over there. He'll see you!"

"I'm not looking at him," Ivy said, still looking. "But *you* should be. Oh, he just glanced over here. Drat! Mattie, raise your chin, for heaven's sake. Toss your head. Do something! He'll come over and ask you to dance if you'd at least *smile*."

"I'm not going to simper like a nincompoop," Mattie fumed. She sneaked a peek at the stranger. Her heart seemed to plunge a great distance, maybe all the way to the toes of her too-tight Sunday boots. Sometimes she hated being a girl!

"Besides, he's only got eyes for Jenny Scarborough," she said.

"Where is she?" Ivy asked, turning her head to and fro.

"Don't bother; you can't see her," Mattie grumbled. "You never see Jenny at a dance. You just see the crowd of men clumped around her."

Ivy waved a gloved hand. "Everybody has eyes for Jenny when they first see her," she said. "They can't help it. It's up to you to get him to notice you."

Mattie's eyes narrowed. She would compete in a knife-throwing contest. She'd enter a wood-chopping contest. But she would never, ever compete in a contest for capturing a man's attention. Especially when her competitor was Jenny Scarborough.

Not only was Jenny the prettiest of the brides, she made matters worse by being one of the sweetest-tempered. Even through the steamy heat of Panama and the boredom of the voyage up the coast of California, Jenny had never lost her temper. Her dresses never wilted. She never, ever perspired, and she certainly never swore. Not even when a seagull had made a mess on her best bonnet.

Ivy poked her. "Go on, Mattie. Brush by him and drop a glove or something."

"I'm completely parched with thirst," Mattie complained. "I'm going to fetch some lemonade."

She turned away from the knowing look in her sister's eyes and pushed blindly through the crowd.

She knew that Ivy wanted her to have a beau. Ivy spent much of her time with Justus now. She most likely thought Mattie was lonely.

But Mattie wasn't lonely. Or she *wouldn't* be if her sister didn't keep pointing out how alone she was!

The lemonade stand was crowded with more silly town gentlemen fetching cool drinks for their womenfolk. Mattie avoided it and headed to where she felt most comfortable—with the rough ranchers and miners. They milled around the spot where the horse race would begin later that afternoon.

Still hoping for something to transport, Mattie eavesdropped on the crowd. But everyone was concerned with placing bets on the upcoming race. When the crucial topic of horseflesh was about, men could barely talk of anything else.

Finally Mattie spotted the familiar broad face of Moses Callanan, a horse breeder she knew from outside Sacramento. She'd bought her own horse, Princie, from him. She never failed to stop by his spread when she had a chance.

"Moses!" she called, and waved as he turned around and saw her. He held a fistful of money, and he grinned when he saw Mattie.

"Are you here to put down a bet, young lady?"

"Shame on you, Moses; you know ladies don't do such things," Mattie said.

"Ladies don't drive an old wagon over mountain roads during the February snows, either," Moses said, his eyes twinkling. "But my, Miss Nesbitt, you're looking mighty fetching today. I've yet to see you in a dress."

"My sister insisted," Mattie said, pushing back her bonnet impatiently. "But I'm hoping to pick up a job here. If I find something to haul, would you happen to have a mount I could borrow? I'd pay you for your trouble."

"Now, Miss Mattie, you know I'd do anything for you, especially in that blue gown," Moses replied. "But I only brought Typhoon to the fair. I can't lend out my best mount for a hauling job. And I was hoping to get some offers for him, though it would break my heart to sell him. Still, Mrs. Callanan will be happy. The beast threw me yesterday, and I got a knock on the head. The missus said it was too bad it didn't knock any sense in me."

Mattie smiled. "I understand. I wouldn't take Typhoon, anyway. He's a fine horse."

"Come back and watch the race with me," Moses urged. "I'll find you a good place."

"I'll see," Mattie replied, but Moses was already turning away to take someone's bet.

She walked only a few paces before she saw Justus bearing down on her. He waved at her, and she could see that he had someone in tow. Mattie almost wheeled around to run the other way, but it was too late.

It was the aloof stranger! And by the look of his scowl, he was none too pleased to find himself dragged behind Justus.

Quickly Mattie tilted her bonnet back down to shade her eyes. Thoughts of murder were in her heart as a beaming Justus hurried up to her.

"Mattie, I want you to meet a friend of mine. This is Sam Jackson Brand," he said proudly. "Sam, this is Miss Mattie Nesbitt."

"Pleased to meet you," Sam Brand said.

"How do you do," Mattie murmured. She kept her eyes downcast. She longed to sneak in a good stomp on Justus's foot.

"I did some legal work for Sam's father," Justus launched out into the dead silence.

"He appreciated all your hard work, sir," Sam Brand said.

"Hey now, I've an idea," Justus said. He widened his green eyes as though the thought had just occurred to him. "Ivy will have my head if I'm not back with her lemonade. Sam, would you be so kind as to escort Miss Nesbitt to the dance floor?"

"Of course," Sam said in the same polite tone.

"And you might want to take a turn," Justus suggested, ignoring the savage look on Mattie's face. "It's a shame to lose the opportunity to dance to such a fine fiddler. I'll hold your bonnet for you, Mattie."

Mattie looked up at Sam Brand's face just in time to see a flash of reluctance. Then the same quiet mask returned.

"I'd be honored," he said with excruciating politeness.

Murder was too good for Justus, Mattie decided. She gave him a baleful look along with her bonnet. He only batted his eyes at her innocently.

She had no choice. Gritting her teeth, Mattie followed an obviously reluctant Sam Jackson Brand to the dance floor. But she made sure to stomp on Justus's foot on the way.

CHAPTER THREE
THE LONGEST WALTZ IN HISTORY

Mattie's bad luck continued when they reached the dance floor. Suddenly the band, which had been playing a lively two-step, settled into a slow, romantic waltz.

She wanted to groan out loud. She could have made it through a quadrille, where she'd swing through several partners as well as Sam. But to have his arms around her as they made slow circles around the dance floor was agony. She'd never survive!

She stepped into Sam's arms. His face was positively grim. He might be attending the funeral of his best friend. He might be facing a hangman's noose.

No. He's just dancing with poor plain old me, Mattie thought bleakly as she placed her hand in his.

Sam rocked back and forth in a motion that was an unpleasant reminder of her bout with seasickness on the trip to California. The motion seemed to be unrelated to the sweet melody of the waltz. He held her stiffly, his eyes fixed at a point over her head.

Mattie bit her lip. He couldn't make it any more obvious that he'd rather be anywhere but where he was.

Maybe a bit of conversation was the way to win him over. "Just try," she heard Ivy urge in her head. "Say something pleasant. Say anything!"

"It's a lovely day," she said. "It was such a hard winter."

"Yes," he said.

Yes! How charming you are, Mr. Brand.

Sam plodded his way through the music. He never looked directly at her. He was probably searching the crowd for Jenny's shining blond head.

Mattie decided on a plan to get back at her meddling sister and her future brother-in-law. *The first thing I'll do is lure Ivy to see the view from Devil's Drop. Then I'll take her by her two hands and hang her over the gorge for a few satisfying seconds until she promises never, ever to interfere in my life again.*

Then it will be Justus's turn . . .

Sam let out the tiniest sigh. His breath stirred a curl by her ear. Then he turned left while she swung right, and they missed cracking heads by a fraction. Instead, his lips brushed her hair.

It was a simple, accidental contact. And as contacts go, it wasn't very intimate. But suddenly, Mattie found herself *aware*.

She was conscious of every point of contact between their two bodies. How rough his palm felt against hers. The calluses spoke of hard work, hard riding. One hand rested on her waist. He was barely touching her, but she could feel the warmth of his skin through her dress.

If she shifted her eyes, she had a close-up view of the curve of his ear and his shiny black hair. She could smell him, too, a pleasant scent, a scent of soap and a clean shirt. And something else, too, grass and air and river. He smelled like . . . outdoors, Mattie thought, closing her eyes.

It was the most peculiar sensation. She was nervous, and she was calm. Even while her pulse skittered and scampered, she could now sway gracefully with the music, actually enjoying it instead of enduring it. She enjoyed the feel of Sam's hands, even the rocking motion that passed for a dance step. Sam must have caught her relaxation, for the waltz became less of a plod and more of a dance.

They made slow circles on the planked floor.

Mattie might as well have been somersaulting through space. She felt giddy. Half of her wanted to keep dancing forever, and half of her couldn't wait to run away and think about the experience in private.

As if to grant her wish, the music stopped. Smiling, Mattie tilted her head back to look at Sam. They'd almost been dancing there at the end. Surely he'd felt that same slow enchantment.

His gaze was somewhere around her shoulder as he released her and gave a short bow.

"Thank you for the dance, Miss—"

"Nesbitt," Mattie supplied. But she could tell he wasn't listening.

He offered his arm, and she took it. He led her to Ivy, who was waiting at the edge of the dance floor. Mattie's face burned as he handed her off to her sister like an unwanted package. Like an overdue bill. Like a telegram with extremely bad news . . .

He gave a final short bow and melted into the crowd.

Ivy slipped her arm into Mattie's and hugged it to her side. "You see how much fun these affairs can be if you'll just *participate*?" she said.

"Speaking of participating . . . ," Justus said, appearing at Ivy's side. "Care to take a turn?"

"I'll be right back," Ivy promised Mattie. "Don't

disappear, now. I want to hear all about your dance."

"I'll be here," Mattie lied with a bright, false smile.

Ivy whirled off with Justus, her face alight. Mattie did the only thing it was possible for her to do under these humiliating circumstances. She disappeared.

Alone, away from the crowd, she let out an angry breath that blew the wayward curls off her forehead.

This time, she was angry at herself.

It wasn't Ivy's fault. She was just trying to get Mattie a partner. It wasn't Justus's fault. He would do anything for Ivy.

It was *her* fault for being such a ninny. It was just a dance. Just a boy. It wasn't the end of the world. So one boy didn't fancy her. What difference did it make?

Mattie leaned against the back side of a wooden booth. In front, people lined up to buy small meat pies. They milled about, calling to each other in high excited voices. But behind the row of booths, all was quiet. Here, the meadow was allowed to bloom, wildflowers swaying in the light breeze.

"Sam! Hey, wait up, will you?"

Mattie stiffened. Footsteps stopped just on the

other side of the booth. It couldn't be. She couldn't have the bad luck to find herself on the other side of the booth from the boy who'd just humiliated her.

"What's on your mind, Billy?"

Mattie winced. Even though Sam Brand had hardly spoken a dozen words to her, she'd recognize his low, quiet voice anywhere. Most young men she knew hooted and brayed. Sam's voice was perfectly distinct but close to a murmur.

"Why are you in such an all-fired hurry?" Billy complained. His voice grew teasing. "So why aren't you dancing? Saw you up there."

"Don't care much for it," Sam answered steadily.

If only she could walk away! But if she did, he'd see her. For some reason, Mattie would rather die than have Sam Brand think she was eavesdropping on him. The best thing to do was to stay quiet.

"Now, that's a lie," Billy said pleasantly. "I seen your foot go tapping to a fiddle once or twice."

"Tapping isn't dancing," Sam replied. "Besides, there's only one girl here worth dancing with."

Mattie gave up any thoughts of fleeing. She strained her ears to catch every one of Sam's soft words.

"And she doesn't lack for partners," Sam continued.

"I believe I know who you're referring to," Billy

said. Mattie could hear the grin in his voice. "It's that Jenny Scarborough, isn't it?"

"Who else?" Sam said. "She's the prettiest girl in three counties."

"Man alive, Sam, there's more than one way to skin a cat," Billy replied. "And there's more than one girl to dance with. There's a passel of pretty girls here."

"I haven't seen any."

"Look at that meadow, there," Billy said. "There's some bluebells and some daisies and some cowbells—you can't tell me one's prettier than another."

Sam let out a snort. "There's wildflowers and there's wallflowers," he said.

Mattie's cheeks burned. Tears spurted to her eyes. If she'd felt humiliated before, now she was devastated.

Wallflower!

Hot tears spilled down Mattie's cheeks. She felt as though she couldn't breathe. Her only relief came when she heard Sam and his companion head back into the crowd.

Mattie didn't hesitate. Swiping at her tears angrily, she took off across the meadow. The hem of her skirt dragged in the mud, but she didn't care. She ran and ran until she thought her heart might burst. She didn't stop until she had crossed the meadow and ended up in a cool grove of trees.

She sank down against the trunk of a tall pine. She stuck out her legs and regarded her muddy kid boots, exhausted. Through the red haze of confusion and shame, she latched on to one emotion: cool fury at Sam Jackson Brand.

What kind of a person could be so casually cruel?

A mean person, that's who.

Mattie regarded the blue dress Ivy had made for her. She hated it now. She had felt pretty in it. Foolish Mattie, who thought she could put on a pretty dress and make herself into the kind of girl boys liked.

Well, she was tired of trying to be a girl. She'd never been good at it. She still wasn't good at it. Despite Ivy's best efforts, she would always fall short.

Mattie stood up and dusted off her skirt, now stained with grass, pine needles, and dirt. She strode off, determined to put Sam Brand out of her mind. And to get comfortable.

She walked to where they'd left the buggy. The man in charge of it was napping in the sun.

There was nothing she wanted more than to drive straight back to Last Chance. But Mattie settled for grabbing her work clothes from underneath the seat. She headed for the woods to change.

Minutes later, she felt herself again. Mud could splash on her work boots, and she didn't care. Her large-brimmed hat did a much better job of keeping the sun out of her eyes.

She balled up the blue gown and her petticoat and shoved them under the seat. Ivy would have a fit. But that would be later. Now Mattie could finally enjoy herself.

She headed back toward where the men were milling. The horse race was about to begin.

"Now, there's the Mattie I recognize." Moses Callanan appeared at her side and clapped her on the back.

She grinned. "Thought I'd get comfortable. Ready for the race?"

"Guess so," Moses replied, frowning. "But my rider never showed up. I sure wish my wife wasn't here today. I could ride Typhoon myself. That's the way to show her off, in a race. But the wife would catch me up, for sure. What a fine animal! The horse, I mean," Moses added with a laugh. "A bit spooky, but the best ones are nervous. I call it spirit."

"Why don't I ride her?" Mattie suggested.

"You?" Moses looked surprised.

Mattie put her hands on her hips. "And why not? You've seen me ride."

"True," Moses said, licking his lips thoughtfully. "And I still have time to make a bet on Typhoon."

"Saddle her up, then," Mattie said cheerfully, "and I'll win the race for you."

"You're on," Moses agreed.

Mattie waited under the shade of a tree until Moses had placed new bets. Then he led the horse over to her.

"Easy now," he told her. "Remember, she's skittish."

"I remember," Mattie said. She mounted, talking all the while to the horse in a low voice. She patted her neck. Typhoon pranced a few steps to the right, then seemed to settle as she got used to Mattie's weight.

Mattie walked Typhoon to the starting line. She hoped Ivy was still dancing. If her sister saw her now, she'd come running and yank her right off the horse.

Mattie eased Typhoon in line next to a magnificent black mare. She was so busy clucking to Typhoon, soothing her, that she didn't get a chance to look at the other riders.

But when she looked over at the rider of the black horse, she started. It was Sam!

Typhoon shied, and she quickly bent her will to

gentling her. If she could have taken off, she would have. But the race was about to start. Tugging the brim of her hat low over her forehead, Mattie bent over Typhoon's neck. Her eyes were straight ahead, and she hoped Sam's were, too. She wouldn't want him to see her.

But a smile crept over Mattie's intent face. Actually, she didn't mind Sam being in the race at all. Because she might not impress him on the dance floor, but this was her turf. She was going to beat him. Mister Samuel Jackson Brand was about to get the ride of his life.

CHAPTER FOUR
MAY THE BEST MAN WIN

Mattie had always loved fast horses. And back in Maine, she had even been lucky enough to find someone who shared her passion.

Dr. Will Calvert was sixty-one years old and a widower. He had retired to breed horses, and he welcomed young Mattie onto his farm anytime. Better than that, he let her ride astride and didn't tell her parents. It was proper for ladies to ride sidesaddle.

Dr. Calvert's farm was where Mattie had learned to ride. Not in a demure sidesaddle, jogging down a smooth path, but fast, flat out, across meadows, over fences, and crashing through streams. Having a business hauling mail over the rough California roads had only improved her riding skills. The quicker she rode, the more runs she could do, and the more money she made.

Typhoon pranced by the starting line, proud,

impatient. She soothed her with gentle words and a pat on her flank.

"On your mark, gentlemen—"

"Shhh," Mattie cooed into Typhoon's ear.

"Set—"

She tensed her knees, feeling Typhoon's powerful muscles vibrate with strain. She pulled back on the reins—

The gun went off, Mattie urged Typhoon, and the horse surged forward. It was all confusion at the starting line as everyone jockeyed for position. Dust and mud flew, curses rang through the air, hooves pounded, horses jostled, and the crowd roared.

Mattie kept her head down and concentrated on keeping as straight a line as she could. The trick to winning a race was to stake out a position and hold to it, no matter how much another rider crowded you. Somewhere off to the side she sensed Sam on the big black horse, but she pushed the knowledge aside. She would have time to look later.

The course was a rough one, down the main street of town, across pastures, around a farm, and across a rutted field before looping back toward the fairground. Mattie was glad she knew the town of Grass Valley fairly well. She was able to follow the marked-out course and keep at a pounding gallop.

Riders fell away behind her. With the wind in her face and only the sound and feel of the horse underneath her straining toward the same goal, Mattie felt exhilaration sweep over her. She was going to win!

But she was aware of a shadow at her shoulder. A shadow that grew with each yard gained. As Typhoon leaped a fence and splashed through a stream, the shadow took the form of a black horse and its rider. Together they were a seamless image of motion, boy and horse, as they took the same obstacles as she without stopping, gaining an inch and another inch and a foot and a yard, until they were neck and neck. She could feel his determination to win pitted against hers, and she gritted her teeth and urged Typhoon on.

The home stretch was ahead, a good five hundred yards of flat-out meadow. Mattie hugged Typhoon's neck, urging the horse on with hoarse voice and knees and pure will. But Sam was with her, keeping pace, drawing ahead, drawing behind, as they thundered toward the last few feet.

For a moment, she thought she was going to win it. But Sam and his horse, in a sudden, impressive burst of speed, forged ahead of her by just a length and crossed the finish line first.

She rose a bit in the saddle and let Typhoon have

her head, cantering until the horse had a chance to calm down. Sam was just ahead.

What did he think of her now? she wondered, cool wind against hot cheeks. The girl who he'd been forced to dance with had come within a hair of beating him, fair and square.

When he cantered back in her direction, the crowd spilled past the finish line and gathered around him. Sam gentled his horse to a walk. He slid down to be clapped on the back and congratulated. Mattie watched him as he nodded, shook hands, and dusted off his pant legs with his hat.

The mayor of Grass Valley hurried forward and presented him with the prize, a gleaming leather saddle. Sam accepted it with the same calm good nature as he'd accepted the congratulations. He allowed himself to be clapped on the back one more time and then disappeared into the crowd.

So he wouldn't see her, after all.

Perhaps it was just as well. Because she didn't beat him. She *almost* did. And in Mattie's opinion, almost only counted in horseshoes.

Now disappointed, Mattie looped Typhoon's reins around her wrist and went looking for Moses. He must still have been settling bets, for she couldn't find him in the crowd.

"Congratulations, mate," a voice said. A too-vigorous hand clapped her back, almost sending her to her knees.

Mattie turned. "Thanks," she said absently, still searching for Moses.

"That was some good hard riding," the man said. He was short and stocky, with a black beard. His arm muscles bulged underneath his flannel shirt.

Mattie gave another short nod. She was tired, and she desperately wanted some water.

"You about five-two, five-three?" he asked.

Surprised, Mattie nodded. "Five-two," she said.

"Couple pounds shy of one hundred, I reckon," he mused, eyeing her.

"I beg your pardon," Mattie said. "I don't see—"

"I'm a scout for the Pony Express," the man interrupted. "Name's Halliday. Saw you ride and thought, well, there's a perfect candidate right there. We're looking for riders who can go fast over hard roads. Pay is one hundred twenty-five dollars a month. You interested?"

The Pony Express! Stunned, Mattie couldn't reply for a moment. The service had just started up in April, and already everyone knew about the daring riders.

What a life it must be, Mattie thought excitedly.

Instead of poking along in an old wagon, she could be flying down a mountainside in a rushing blaze of glory!

"Hey, Mattie! There you are!" Moses appeared with a cry and a grin. He picked her up and swung her around. Mattie's hat flew off and her auburn hair tumbled down her back. "What a ride, girl! What a ride! I got buyers lined up to look at Typhoon. I just won a hundred dollars on you, and here's a ten-dollar gold piece to thank you for it." He tucked it into the palm of her hand. "Just don't tell my wife I was betting."

"Girl?" Halliday said in amazement. He took off his hat and scratched his head. "Well, I'll be. That's a joke on me, I reckon." He took out a cigar from his pocket and put it, unlit, in his mouth. He looked Mattie up and down. "That's one on me," he repeated slowly. "Sorry about that, missy."

"Don't be sorry about it," Mattie said. "I'm interested in the job."

He laughed.

"I am," Mattie insisted. "I'm the same person who just ran that race, Mr. Halliday."

"She's a goldurned fine rider, Mr. Whoever You Are," Moses said, his happy face pink with excitement. "If you're looking for somebody to do a job, you can't do better than Mattie." Giving her a final pat on the shoulder, he took Typhoon's reins from her and led the horse away.

"There's a big difference between running a race and riding through snowdrifts chest-high," Halliday said with a patronizing smile that made Mattie want to smack him. "Or splashing around in icy streams or dodging hostile Indians. You wouldn't be riding down familiar lanes. You'd be tackling a hundred-mile journey over hazardous terrain."

"But I *could* do all that!" Mattie cried. "Why, I already do! I—"

"Now, don't get excited there, missy," Halliday said. "I'm not saying you're not a good rider. But I can't use you, and that's that." He tipped his hat. "You have a good afternoon, now."

Furious, her heart full of angry things she burned to say, Mattie watched him walk away. Standing straight and silent, just like a girl. Like a polite, dutiful girl.

CHAPTER FIVE
IN WHICH MATTIE CUTS HER HAIR

Mattie told herself she was happy to get back to Last Chance. Happy to get back to her work. Happy to be riding along in her wagon, just as she should be.

But she wasn't. Not at all. Everything had changed since the fair in Grass Valley. Suddenly everything seemed . . . flat.

She wasn't happy hauling mail. She wasn't happy walking through a mountain meadow. She wasn't happy joking with the other girls at the boardinghouse, and she wasn't even happy sitting with her hot tea in the morning on Annie's back porch, watching the mist lift off the mountains.

Nothing that used to make her happy did so anymore. Mattie had puzzled over this for some time. She'd never been unhappy before, just because of something little. She'd been through bad times in Maine, awful times. Her father had been disgraced when he'd embezzled money from the bank in order to save her aunt's farm. She'd been miserable then, but she hadn't been so all-fired *gloomy*.

And when he'd died, she'd been full of sorrow and grief, but she hadn't been so mad at herself, so dad-blamed itchy.

So unhappy with herself, Mattie admitted.

The fair had cruelly pointed out to her that she wasn't one thing or another. She didn't make a decent girl. She couldn't capture a man's attention, or even be clever enough to amuse one for the length of a dance.

But the race had taught her that she didn't belong in a masculine world, either. She could ride well and shoot straight and even cuss under extreme provocation (as long as Ivy wasn't around). She could do anything a boy her age could do *except* get a job he could get. Simply because of her sex.

Mattie had been slapped in the face with the injustice of being a girl plenty of times before. But this was like being conked on the head with an anvil.

First she got rejected for not being pretty enough. Then she got rejected for not being tough enough. She didn't belong anywhere. And that was the loneliest feeling in the world.

The gloom didn't lift on her usual Wednesday trip

to Sacramento. It was an easy wagon trip on a good road, but Mattie couldn't enjoy it. She kept remembering the Pony Express scout's patronizing smile.

She kicked the wagon in frustration. She felt as though she were inching along today. She could be racing on a powerful horse, the wind in her face. It was so unfair to be offered freedom and adventure and have it snatched from her grasp!

Mattie delivered her packages in Sacramento, some to the steamship that would carry them to San Francisco, and a bundle of packages to Opal Pollard's sister. Ruby gave her a package to take back to Opal, some material she'd found for summer dresses.

Mattie tucked the brown paper package under her arm. She refused Ruby's usual offer of lemonade and walked back to the livery stable where she'd left her wagon. She paused to stare out at the river and catch the breeze. When in tarnation would she get out of this head-scratching, stomach-turning, irritating, unaccountable *mood*?

Then, across the street, she saw it—the Pony Express office. Dodging wagons and ignoring a startled "hey!" from a driver, Mattie hurried across the street.

She paused outside to read the paper plastered

to the grimy wooden face of the building.

Wanted: Riders. Young, skinny, wiry, not over eighteen. Must be expert riders willing to risk death daily. Orphans preferred.

The words drummed in her head. She wanted to stamp her feet and howl. But a delicious piece of knowledge teased her brain. Nowhere in the ad did it mention they wanted *males*.

She was young, skinny, wiry, and an expert rider. Next to Ivy and her aunt Pru back in Maine, she didn't have kin. If anyone fit the description, she did.

Filled with purpose now, Mattie strode down the walk, her eyes searching the building signs aside. When she saw what she wanted, she gave a cry of satisfaction and entered.

A few minutes later, she took her purchases into an alley. She unwrapped a small mirror and balanced it on a crate. Then she took out the scissors and untied the thong that held her hair back.

It tumbled around her shoulders, catching the sunlight and flashing red and gold. Mattie sighed. Her hair had always been her secret pride. It was thick and wavy, the color of an autumn leaf. But she hesitated for only a moment.

She picked up a thick plait and snipped it off. It dropped into the mud.

"You see?" she said through gritted teeth. "It didn't hurt, you ninny."

Slowly she hacked away at her beautiful hair until it littered the dirt at her feet. Shorn, she regarded herself.

She had the same blue eyes, the same five freckles scattered on her nose. Her face had never had the soft, round qualities she'd admired in other girls. Now its angularity would help her. She jammed her hat back on her head and squinted.

A boy stared back. Mattie pitched her voice low. "Hey," she grunted. "Name's Matt."

Whistling, Mattie jammed the mirror and scissors into her leather saddlebag and slung it over her shoulder. She'd become a boy in her own eyes. Now she'd see if it would work on others.

She returned to the Pony Express office. Before she could lose her nerve, she grabbed the knob of the door and turned. She clomped inside, and the clerk looked up questioningly.

Mattie pitched her voice low and told herself to sound gruff. To be almost rude, like a young man would. She should make a demand, not a request.

"I come for a job," she said.

CHAPTER SIX
A BARGAIN

"Absolutely not," Ivy said firmly. "I won't hear of it."

"Surely we can discuss—"

"No," Ivy said, turning her back. "We cannot. I'm still your guardian, Mattie. You're only seventeen."

"And you're only eighteen! It isn't fair!"

Ivy picked up her sewing. "It doesn't matter if it's fair or not. I'm not sending you off to be a Pony Express rider, and that's that."

"But I already accepted the job!" Mattie protested, her blue eyes stormy.

Ivy looked up at her younger sister. Her heart hurt for her. Just looking at Mattie's poor cropped head could bring tears to Ivy's eyes. It was proof of how unhappy she was, how desperate to break out of her life.

"Sit down, dear," she said softly. She patted the sofa next to her.

Reluctantly, Mattie threw herself down next to Ivy. For once Ivy didn't criticize her for not seating herself like a lady. She stroked her shorn hair.

"Don't you see, you silly, how I couldn't bear it if anything happened to you?" Ivy said softly. "You're all I have. It's always been the two of us. I couldn't do without you."

Mattie leaned against her sister. Ivy had sent a cunning shaft straight to her own weakness. Everything Ivy said was in Mattie's heart, too. She and Ivy were family. They had been through so much—the death of their mother, their father's disgrace, his heart attack, and the poverty he'd left them with. They had pulled each other through, step by agonizing step. She couldn't bear it if anything happened to Ivy. She supposed she should understand her sister's feelings.

"I feel the same, and you know it," she answered her sister in the same quiet tone. "But when you told me you were to marry Jamie Rayburne and sail off to the South Seas, I didn't try to stop you. It was breaking my heart not to beg you to stay, but I didn't."

"You were always stronger than me," Ivy said. "And besides, it wasn't your place to object. I'm *your* guardian, remember?"

"Oh, foot," Mattie said helplessly. Ivy had an answer for everything.

Ivy picked up her sewing again. "It's too dangerous, Mattie. Bad enough that you go tearing around the mountains in that old wagon. But the Express is fifty times more dangerous. You have to worry about marauding Paiutes and sudden floods and those isolated stations. Not to mention what might happen if those ruffians find out you're a girl." Ivy shuddered. "No, it is much too dangerous."

"But Ivy, think of the chance!" Mattie pleaded. "I was lucky to get the job, first of all. And I'd only be a relief rider—that's all they had. If only I'd gone the day after the fair!" She saw by the exasperation in Ivy's eyes that she'd gone on the wrong track.

"But as a relief rider, I'd only work for two months," she continued. "The regular boy broke his leg—"

Ivy shuddered, and Mattie saw that she had made another misstep.

"Anyway, it would only be for two months," she said again, deflated.

"That's two months too long," Ivy said. "No."

Mattie's jaw set stubbornly. "I could just go, you know."

Ivy looked at her over the handkerchief she was embroidering. Her amber eyes were serious. "I know that," she said quietly. "I know I can't keep you, Mattie. But I would hope that my strong opposition would be enough to stop you from a course such as this. Just as yours would stop me. I have respect for your judgment, and I hope you have the same respect for mine."

"But you *don't* have respect for mine!" Mattie argued. "If you did, you'd let me go!"

Ivy's lips pressed together, but she didn't speak. Ivy hated to argue. And she hated to disappoint Mattie. The two sisters were silent. The only sound was the *plunk* of Ivy's needle through the material.

Mattie threw her head back against the parlor sofa. She regarded the ceiling with bleak eyes. Going off without Ivy's blessing had been an empty threat. She couldn't cross her sister that way. She had to think of a sound reason to sway Ivy. To Mattie, disguising herself as a boy and becoming a Pony Express rider was a grand adventure. It was like a story she'd stay up at night to finish reading. A story her sister might write . . .

Mattie sat up. "I'm surprised at you, Ivy," she said. "Disappointed as well."

"Disappointed?" Ivy looked up.

"You've always championed the rights of women," Mattie said. "Weren't you reading to me about Elizabeth Cady Stanton the other day?"

"Mrs. Stanton is doing important work," Ivy said. "She's not wearing trousers and racing all over the country."

"But she supports my right to do so!" Mattie argued. She thumped the seat of the sofa. "She supports the rights of women. The right to do a job as well as any man, if that is her inclination!"

One corner of Ivy's mouth lifted in an ironic smile. "Are you having a conversation with me or giving a speech?"

"Ivy, don't you think it a terrible wrong to be offered a job and then have it taken away strictly because of your sex?"

Reluctantly, Ivy nodded. "Of course I do, Mattie, but—"

"Don't you think it would strike a blow for women in California—for women everywhere—if they knew that a *female* had successfully done one of the most dangerous and rigorous jobs in the West?"

"Well, yes, but—"

Eagerly, Mattie twisted on the sofa to face her sister. "Ivy, we see it every day here in California.

Women are prospectors and farmers and ranchers. Yet men can always make excuses for them when they're successful. They can say that they were lucky, or they had the help of a man. Don't you despise that in your very soul?"

"Of course I do!" Ivy exclaimed. "It's insufferable."

"Think, Ivy," Mattie said, grasping her sister's hands. "Think what a blow you could strike for all of us if you told my story. You know I can do it; you know I can ride as well as any man. You know I have the energy and the courage."

Ivy looked into her sister's blazing eyes. "I do know that," she admitted in a gentle voice.

"And you know that denying me this chance would break my heart," Mattie said. "Oh, I would never hold it against you, Ivy, you know that. I love you too well. But I would shrivel up inside if I didn't get a chance to *try*."

Tears came to Mattie's eyes. "I want to belong somewhere, Ivy."

Ivy bit her lip. She felt the strength of her sister's grip as Mattie squeezed her hands. There were times she missed her mother so! She didn't know what to advise Mattie. She didn't want to hold her back, but she was afraid for her.

But Mattie wasn't afraid. There was no fear in her.

She had always been different that way. Ivy always had to struggle against fear. Mattie never felt it at all.

She was her own woman. Perhaps Ivy didn't have a right to forbid Mattie anything. Perhaps she couldn't. Perhaps Mattie would always be striding forward, out of her grasp. Ivy couldn't protect her. And she couldn't hold her back.

Mattie saw the weakening in Ivy's eyes. Triumph surged through her, but she didn't show it.

"Two months," Ivy said helplessly. "I'll give you two months. That's all. Long enough to prove a woman can do the job. Long enough to prove it to yourself. I'll hold you to that promise, Mattie."

Mattie squeezed her hands again, making Ivy wince. "I won't let you down."

Mattie was up at dawn the next morning. There was so little to pack. One change of clothes. A blanket. A revolver. Mattie tucked it underneath her clothes so that Ivy wouldn't see it.

Her home station would be Friday's Station on the eastern side of the Sierra. Her route would take her through the Nevada Territory, passing through Genoa and Carson City until she reached her other home station of Fort Churchill, where she would rest before starting back.

Ivy waited for Mattie in the dark front hall. She drew her shawl closely around her, though she wasn't really cold. She wanted to hold her sister to her and ask her again to change her mind, but she didn't.

Mattie strode in the hall, carrying her saddlebags and hat. Ivy looked at her and knew that though her sister was sad to leave her, she was anxious to be gone. Every line of her body spoke of her impatience, her excitement. She was heading off to a grand adventure.

"Remember," Mattie said. "You'll get a good story out of this. Maybe your best."

Tears sprang to Ivy's eyes. "Oh, Mattie. I would give up a hundred good stories just to have you safe."

"Oh, Ivy," Mattie said. "I'm certain I'll have more stories to give you than a hundred!"

Laughter bubbled out of Ivy, despite the tears in her eyes. She hugged Mattie fiercely.

"God bless you."

Mattie found a lump in her throat that she couldn't quite speak around. She could only nod, put on her hat, and go.

CHAPTER SEVEN
WAKING THE SNAKE

Mattie paced back and forth on the porch of the Express station, her boots thudding on the splintered wood. Her eyes scanned the horizon for dust, the first sign that a rider was approaching. Her heart was beating in a quick rhythm, and she ran her perspiring hands down her pants. It wouldn't do at all if the reins slipped out of her wet hands and she flew off her horse on her very first run!

Everything was in place. Her horse stood waiting. On the horse's back was a specially designed saddle, lighter in weight with a short horn. When the rider dismounted, he would throw the *mochila*—the soft leather pouch with four pockets that contained the mail—over her saddle. And she would be off.

Her total equipment could weigh only thirteen pounds, and that included her revolver and saddle. Letters were written on special tissue paper to save weight. Everything—rider, horse, saddle, even the mail itself—was designed for speed.

For her eighty-five-mile run to Fort Churchill in the Utah Territory, she would change horses at "swing stations" four times. She would go at a full gallop the whole time, as fast as she dared.

"You're going to wear out the porch boards if you keep up that pacing. A mite jumpy, are you?"

It was Del, the assistant to the station manager, Alfie Wilkes. Del was a large, lumbering boy a few years older than she. He had only grunted a hello the morning she'd arrived and had gone about his chores silently. She was surprised to hear him address her.

Mattie gave a shrug. She hated when people saw how nervous she was. And she had told herself to speak as little as possible. The less she spoke, the less chance there was that she'd be discovered.

"Don't blame you at all. First ride's the hardest," Del observed, leaning against the porch post. "Every time there's an accident, it's a first-time rider."

"Shut your mouth, Del," Alfie Wilkes said in a pleasant voice as he checked for the second time to make sure Mattie's saddle was cinched. "You're just mad because you're too big and fleshy to ride."

Del's face flushed an angry red. "I wouldn't be blame-fool enough to be a rider. I'm smarter than that."

Smarter? Mattie turned her head to scan the horizon. Her mouth itched to form a wisecrack. It would serve Del right. But she had to screen out everything except the ride ahead.

Instead, she started to pace again. This time, as she passed Del, she tripped over his foot. She knew he'd stuck it out on purpose. She nearly went flying, but she caught herself on the porch rail.

"I didn't do nothing," Del whined.

Mattie flushed with anger. She knew it would be dangerous to get in a war of words with Del. She knew how boys were. Sooner or later, it would escalate into a physical fight, and then she'd be in trouble. She'd just have to ignore him.

"Del, I told you to leave the boy be!" Alfie yelled irritably. "We don't want to be short a rider! Get inside where you belong. Matt, stay away from that son of a—*head's up!*"

Alfie's practiced eye had glimpsed the dust on the horizon. In another minute, they could hear the faint pounding of hooves.

Mattie mounted her horse. Every muscle in her body tightened. Everything in the world faded away except that tiny black speck. In less time than she'd dreamed possible, the rider was upon them, swinging off his horse, grabbing the *mochila,* and expertly tossing it over the pommel of her saddle. She caught a flash of the other rider's dirt-encrusted face and his grin.

It was Sam Brand.

She lost her bearings for a moment. She saw the same recognition in his eyes, the same surprise.

But there was no time to react. Mattie grabbed the reins and kicked the horse, shouting a version of "*giddyap!*" and taking off. In moments she was streaming down the road, up to a full-out gallop.

She didn't know if her heart was pounding from excitement or fear. Would Sam reveal her true identity? He had most assuredly recognized her. Hadn't he?

But Mattie didn't have time or leisure to wonder about Sam. The road took all her attention. At this speed, every rut was a hazard. She had to watch for slow-moving carts, reckless stage drivers, gopher holes—anything and everything became a danger.

Mattie had time to think of nothing but her body and the horse and the mail. Her nerves were pitched high, her body taut with effort. At every swing station she had no time to even greet the manager, so intent was she upon swinging the *mochila* over the next saddle, mounting the next horse, and urging him into a full gallop.

Genoa. Carson City. Dayton. Reed's Station. She counted off the stations, swung herself back in the saddle, kept going, never stopping, never slackening.

There was only pounding hooves and screaming nerves. There was only sky and rushing ground, sagebrush, dirt and mud. There was only effort, and at the last, there was only will.

A misty moon rose in a purpling sky. She streaked past blurs that could be sagebrush or feeding mule deer. She was tired to the bone but had no time to consider it.

At last the adobe of Fort Churchill rose ahead. She saw the rider waiting, saw him wave a short greeting. And she was off her horse, flinging the mail over the next saddle, and stumbling backward to fall on her knees.

"First runs are the hardest."

Mattie looked up into the creased face of the station tender. She only had the strength to nod.

"I'm Charley Goodnight. Come on inside; I'll fix you up with some food."

Mattie stumbled behind him. She fell on the plate of beans and some unidentifiable meat like a starving dog.

"Name's Matt Nesbitt," she said. "Thanks for the food."

Charley nodded. "Your bunk's over there," he said, nodding at a pallet in the corner. "You can wash up out back."

Mattie swallowed a mouthful of beans. Her bed was right out in the open. How was she going to manage getting undressed?

She'd just have to, that's all. She'd sleep in her dusty clothes. Because she wasn't going to let a little inconvenience stand between her and this job. She was worn out, grimy, and jounced to pieces. And she'd never had such fun in her life.

Once she sat on her bunk, she found she only had strength enough to take off her boots. With an *oof*, she drew up the thin blanket around her and crashed onto her back.

Charley chuckled. "You'll get used to it, in time."

"Sure hope so," Mattie mumbled.

But she felt fine. She'd had one rip-roaring ride, and she'd brought the mail through. Annie Friend would say that she'd gone and "waked the snake" by posing as a boy. She'd set herself up for a mess of trouble, she supposed. And she wasn't even thinking of the riding. Hard as it was, it was the easiest part.

It was always people who messed things up, Mattie thought tiredly. Del could be a problem. And then there was Sam.

He could ruin everything. Would he keep her secret? The question hung in her brain as she drifted off to a deep sleep. Would he tell Alfie and Del that the new rider was the girl he'd danced with at the Grass Valley fair?

When she returned to Friday's Station, would she be out of the best job she'd ever had?

CHAPTER EIGHT
RIVALS

Thirty-six hours of rest and she was back in the saddle. This time, Mattie felt more confident. She already knew the dangers. She knew how she'd have to push her body to sheer exhaustion. And she knew when the ride ended there would be rest and the feeling of a hard job done well.

She pounded into Friday's Station at a full gallop and swung the pouch full of mail over the saddle of the waiting horse. There was just a flicker of an unreadable expression on Sam Brand's face, but she had no time to puzzle it out. He galloped off, leaving her choking on his dust.

She cast a nervous eye at Alfie Wilkes. Del led her horse off to tend it. Had Sam told them she was a girl? Or was he keeping the information to himself until he could confront her with it? He seemed like the type to keep his own counsel.

"Got some stew on," Alfie said.

She nodded, relieved. She took off her hat and ran her hand through her short coppery hair. It felt stiff with sweat and caked with dirt. Ivy would be horrified.

He set a tin plate heaped with stew and bread in front of her. "I've been hearing about you from Sam," he said. "You been keeping secrets, have you?"

Her mouth stuffed with bread, Mattie's blue eyes went wide. Alfie's back was to her as he poured out a mug of coffee from the pot.

He turned and placed it in front of her. Mattie found it difficult to swallow. She took a quick sip of the scalding brew to soften the bread.

"Sam told me you came right close to beating him in the Grass Valley race," Alfie said. His small dark eyes crinkled. "If I'd have come close to beating Sam Brand, I wouldn't be keeping it a secret."

Mattie swallowed with a gulp. The coffee burned down her throat, and tears came to her eyes.

"Coffee does get hot," Alfie said kindly. "You better sip it slow."

The coffee had burned, but it was more than that. Would Sam Brand ever stop humiliating her? Mattie wondered.

He didn't remember her as a girl at all! Not as a girl he'd held in his arms, a girl he'd danced with for long minutes. He remembered her as a boy he'd barely glimpsed once! Just because that boy had almost beaten him in a race, *his* image was burned into Sam's memory.

"Weren't nothing," Mattie mumbled, her head down over her bowl.

Del stomped into the station. "Yeah, that's what Sam said," he chortled, pouring himself a cup of coffee.

She eyed him. "What *did* Sam say?" she asked gruffly.

"He didn't say anything," Alfie said. "That's not Sam's way. Del, go swill your dang coffee on the porch, will you? You try my nerves, boy."

Mattie finished her dinner, then took her cup of coffee and joined Del. He looked up at her sulkily from his seat on the stairs.

She leaned on the post. "So what did Sam say?" she asked casually.

Del gave her a sly look. "Just that he wasn't quite up to snuff that day, owing to the fact that he barely got three hours' sleep the night before. Else he would have run you into the ground."

Mattie gripped her cup. What an arrogant, conceited, pompous boor Sam was! He was positively a buffoon. He couldn't even admit that someone had almost beat him, fair and square.

"Well," she drawled, "I don't know about the benefits of a good night's sleep, but I figure an Express rider shouldn't complain about such things. All I know is, I was on an unfamiliar mount, and Sam was on his own horse. If I was to make excuses—which *I* never would do, not like some—I'd say if there was a fellow who had an edge, it would be the fellow on his own horse. Wouldn't say it, though. It would look like I was making excuses."

Del grinned, his small dark eyes almost disappearing in his large face. "You got a funny way of talking, Matt. But I get you, all right."

Mattie tossed the rest of Alfie's awful coffee into the dust. That should fix Sam Brand.

When she got back to the station three days later, Del was waiting with an expectant gleam in his eye.

"Sam says it's a dirty varmint who can make an excuse for himself while saying he's not. A good rider should be fast on any horse, Sam says."

Mattie bent over to take off her boots. Exhaustion made her very bones ache, but anger surged through her, giving her energy enough to hurl her boot across the room.

"I could beat Sam Brand riding a mule," she scoffed. "A *lame* mule," she added.

After her next trip, Del was waiting with Sam's response.

"He says that the way you sit a horse, even a mule would refuse to let you ride 'im. You could turn a wild mustang into a pudding foot."

Pudding foot was the term for a clumsy horse that could barely manage a sharp turn. Del let out a strangled giggle as Mattie scowled.

"Sam Brand is awful free with his bragging. Why, anybody could have won that race with that black horse of his," Mattie said scornfully. "The next time my maiden aunt Pru is in town, I'll have her give it a go. I need a new saddle."

Del nodded, his mud brown eyes intent. She knew he was repeating what she'd said to himself, trying to remember it.

She pointed a finger at him. "Now don't you go telling Sam what I said. It seems like the fellow is awful touchy."

Del swallowed his chortle and tried to look trustworthy. "I'll never tell," he promised.

Del told. Sam's comments and Mattie's responses were carried from rider to rider, station tender to station tender. If Mattie had wished to vanish into the corps of Express riders, she was foiled as a fierce rivalry built up between her and Sam. Everyone wanted to know what new insults she and Sam had exchanged.

Now when Sam swung into Friday's Station, he greeted Mattie with a glare. She gave him as good as she got, narrowing her blue eyes and swinging her horse around, nearly stepping on Sam as she did so.

Del was full of sly grins. These days, he willingly poured her coffee and helped her off with her boots. He no longer tried to trip her or questioned her ability to ride. At least something good had come out of her feud with Sam, Mattie reflected. The conflict had almost turned Del into a decent person.

One day, when Mattie pulled up to Friday's Station, an unfamiliar face greeted her. He nodded shortly, already intent on securing the mail and getting off. Where was Sam?

She clomped into the station to find Alfie already pouring her coffee and dishing up his usual stew, which Mattie was convinced he made out of old boots and wild onions.

"Where's Sam?" she asked carelessly, leaning over to splash cold water on her face from the basin. "Did he go and quit on account of me?"

"Had to take some time off," Alfie explained as he set down a plate. "His mother's sick and he has to help with his father's business for a few weeks. His pa owns a store of some kind up on the Columbia River. Used to be a beaver trapper. Anyway, Sam found a substitute to ride for him while he's gone."

Mattie wiped her face and slung the thin towel back on the hook. It dangled sloppily, but she forced herself not to straighten it. That was something a girl would do.

And a girl would be asking questions now. She'd be concerned. She'd ask how poorly Sam's mother was, ask what illness she had. But men didn't ask questions of each other. They accepted facts at face value. They would figure if Sam was gone, someone would replace him, and there was no never mind to them.

Mattie spooned up her first bite of Alfie's awful stew. The trouble was, she wasn't a boy. She was a girl. Which meant that even though she thought Sam was a low-down dirty snake, she was concerned for him. It was only human.

"I had a talk with him before he left," Del said, sitting down at the rough planked table. "We were thinking it was time to nip this thing between you two in the bud."

"What were you thinking?" Mattie asked flippantly, reaching for the bread. "A duel?"

"A race," Del said. "I got the course picked out already. Right by Lake Bigler, so it's not far. We can do it on your layover, before Sam has to start on his route again."

"Oh," Mattie said. She took a mouthful of stew in order to stall. How could she possibly get out of this?

"What do you say, Matt?" Del asked. Even Alfie looked at her expectantly.

She swallowed. "I get enough riding from this job," she said brusquely.

"Sam thought you'd try and get out of it," Del said. "Said you knew you'd lose. Said you'd blame it on the job, but it'd just be 'cause you were yeller—"

Mattie slapped down her spoon. "He did, did he? Name the place and the time, Del. I'll be there."

Alfie grinned as he tilted his chair back to load his pipe. "And here I thought this job would be dull as sagebrush," he said with great satisfaction.

CHAPTER NINE
SHOWDOWN

They would have to wait to race. Sam would be gone for at least two weeks. Mattie felt a sense of relief as she traveled her regular route. It was a darn sight easier to ride when you weren't occupied with trying to dream up the worst insults you knew.

Although Mattie didn't get to socialize with the other riders, she heard about them. They were all a rough bunch, used to making their own way from a tender age. Many were orphans. It was easy for Mattie to reveal the outlines of her life. They fit so many of the other boys'. A mother lost at an early age, a father felled by financial forces and his own folly. Only a sister and a maiden aunt left in the family. Not too many to mourn should Matt Nesbitt take an arrow in the chest or find himself dying from exposure or a fall.

They were all as young as she was, some even younger. At eighteen, Sam was older than most, and he was one of the tallest. Sam made up for his greater height and weight with a speed and grit that were becoming legendary.

There had not been one failure to get the mails through as yet. Each trip was a battle, for failure anywhere along the line could mean that they would not make their ten-day schedule. No one wanted to be responsible for the first failure, and all eighty riders were fiercely dedicated to their task.

But there was still time to think. Time on the layover, after she'd tossed the mail to rider Bob Haslam at Fort Churchill and fell on her food. Time before sleep, when she lay awake on a hard cot and had a few seconds of awareness before succumbing to a dreamless sleep.

And there was time as she rode along her route among the juniper and the piñon pines, when the image of Sam rose in her head, and she couldn't push it away. She would weaken, and she would think again of how his palm had fitted against hers. She could almost recapture that sense of longing she'd had in his arms, a longing that was so close to pain she wondered why she'd wanted to keep feeling it.

She had felt so much, and he had felt so little. She thought of some day, in the distant future, when Mother Nature would take pity on her. Wasn't

Nature a woman? Wouldn't she be kind and some-
day make Mattie lovely?

Half-dreaming in her bunk, Mattie saw herself in
a white dress with a blue sash. She would have hair
that curled just so and round pink cheeks. She
would meet a man's frank gaze without blushing,
without looking at the ground. She saw a day when
she would be able to toss her head and flirt without
feeling a prize fool.

And on that day, she would somehow meet Sam
Jackson Brand again. This time, he would gaze at
her with longing. His eyes would burn as he took in
a figure suddenly womanly, suddenly full of allure.
He would bow. He would say, "Miss Nesbitt, would
you do me the great honor of partnering me in a
dance?" His gaze would be full of hope and desire.

And she would spit in his eye.

"Sam's back," Del announced to her one day
when she awoke from a solid twelve-hour sleep.

She was smart enough not to react. Instead, she
stumbled over to the basin to wash. "So?"

"So I figure we should have the race today."

"Today?"

"I got a bet riding on you, Matt," Alfie called over.

Mattie couldn't help grinning as she dried her

face and arms. "And one on Sam, I reckon."

Alfie smiled widely, revealing most of his tobacco-stained teeth. "Well, folks don't call me wise, but they don't call me stupid, neither."

"I'm betting on you, Matt," Del said.

She cast him an amused glance. She didn't believe him for a minute. "I'm sure you are, Del. All right," she said. "Just let me get some grub. I'm ready."

The race was set for three o'clock that afternoon. Mattie rode over with Del, leaving Alfie to watch the station. Sam would meet them there on a horse from the Express, not his own black pony.

A crowd of men had already gathered by the time Mattie and Del arrived. Word had spread, and any western man worth his salt wouldn't pass up a chance to bet on a race.

Mattie's heart did a sudden flip when she glimpsed Sam's familiar figure. She nodded at him, and he nodded back stonily.

"How's your ma?" she asked.

He looked surprised at the question. "Fine," he said shortly.

If she'd had any thoughts of wishing his mother good health, Mattie squelched them. His manner was so cold, almost rude. Sam Brand was clearly not a gentleman. A gentleman was polite, even to rivals.

She turned away from Sam to study the course. Through the trees she caught a flash of deep blue. It was Lake Bigler, which some called by the Indian name Tahoe. Mattie had a fleeting wish for those uncomplicated days when it was just her and her wagon, free to do as she pleased. Right now, she'd be dipping her hot feet in the Alpine lake and watching the shorebirds. Alone, and happy to be so.

Del's voice jolted her out of her thoughts.

"Starting line's there," he explained, pointing. "It's pretty much a straightaway down the pasture. Turn at that big ol' redwood yonder. Finish line is a hundred yards past that."

Mattie nodded. She jammed her hat further down on her head so that it wouldn't fly off.

"Bill here will start you out," Del said, indicating a burly miner with a cocked revolver.

Mattie and Sam walked their horses to the starting line.

She took a deep breath, trying to calm herself. It wouldn't do her or the horse any good to be nervous.

It all felt so familiar. The sudden silence of the day, the smell of grass and horseflesh. The silent, taut boy beside her.

But this time was different. This time, the race wasn't a lark. It was a deadly contest. And she was going to win.

The gun went off, and they spurred their horses and sprang forward as one. Mattie was used to the sights and smells now. Pounding hooves. Flying dirt. Riding for the Express had only made her faster, keener.

The cries of the men watching came to her faintly. Mattie bent over until her chin brushed her horse's mane. She put everything she had into the race. Every ounce of grit she'd developed over the past weeks, every muscle, every breath.

She pulled ahead. Then Sam inched past her. The trees were a blur. The ground rose and fell. They rounded the corner by the tall redwood. Now there was flat-out riding for the last hundred yards.

Exhilaration roared through her. She was winning, she was winning . . .

And Sam pulled next to her. The miner at the finish line flailed his coat, and it was over. They finished in a dead heat. Nobody had won, and nobody had lost. Never in her life had Mattie felt so cheated.

CHAPTER TEN
FRIENDS

The unhappy faces on the men told Mattie that only a few had bet on the possibility of a dead heat. She saw a number of frustrated exchanges. Money being angrily slapped into palms. Del's face was dark with disappointment. It might be a good time to disappear. She hurried off to drink at the lake.

She stayed for long minutes, splashing water on her face and neck. The next time she saw anyone, she wanted to be composed. She felt just as frustrated as the men who had bet on her.

She had come so close! Mattie smacked the water with the flat of her hand. She should have won. If she'd taken the turn just a mite cleaner . . .

She supposed she should be content with tying with Sam. But Mattie's competitive streak ran wide and deep. She had always wanted to be faster, smarter, cleverer than anybody else. Maybe because she had so much to live up to.

Mattie rocked back on her heels, suddenly plunged into old memories. Her father had been a Latin scholar. Her mother had been not only a beauty but also an accomplished portrait artist. And Ivy had always been . . . well, perfect. Her smooth complexion, shining hair, and graceful manners had set an example for Mattie as soon as she'd been aware.

"Look at your sister," her father would say gently. "Take her as your example." And Mattie would try. But she would always end up slipping somehow, coming in late or disheveled or in disgrace because she'd run races with the boys instead of embroidering samplers with the girls.

Oh, she loved Ivy. Who could not? Her sister had goodness shining out of her very soul. But she'd set an impossible standard of grace and composure. Mattie could never live up to it, so she'd gone a different way. She'd become a rough-and-tumble girl.

She'd been perfectly fine until she was fourteen or so. Then boys started looking at girls in a different way. They cared about how Belinda Royce's curls bounced, not how well Mattie Nesbitt could tie a seaman's knot. They approved of a girl's complexion, not her wisecracks.

She'd always felt out of step, Mattie realized. The feeling hadn't just started at the fair at Grass Valley. It had always been there. And it had made her determined to be as hardy as the boys. As fast, as sure, as defiant.

Mattie sighed and placed her hat on her wet hair. Downstream, she could hear the sound of splashing. She walked a few yards to where trees hid the sandy curve of the lake and saw Sam washing himself in the frigid water. She hurriedly ducked behind the thick screen of the pines.

He had taken off his shirt, and he was beautiful. His skin was brown and glistening. Water ran in rivulets down the compact muscles of his chest.

Mattie ducked behind a tree. She knew she should return to the pasture, but she stayed. She knew she shouldn't be looking, but she looked.

He ducked his whole head in the water and came up, swinging his long hair. It slapped against the smooth skin of his back. She could see the flash of white teeth as he laughed at the shock of the wet cold strands against his flesh.

She was hidden in the shade of the green pines, more shadow than substance, but somehow, he sensed her presence. She saw him tense. Then, incredibly, his eyes met hers. Mattie couldn't believe he could see into shadows so keenly.

"You're still here," he said. Though he was yards away and spoke quietly, his words were distinct and clear.

She didn't say anything. He picked up his shirt and slid into it. It hugged his body, immediately wet. He combed the hair out of his eyes.

"Del took the horses," he said. "I thought you were with him. Guess he was mad at both of us. We'll have to walk back to the station."

Mattie looked back toward the pasture. All she saw was waving grass.

"That buzzard," she said.

"No use bellyaching."

"I'm not bellyaching, I'm just saying—"

"Words won't get us back to town."

"You sure you want to walk with a yellow-bellied coward?"

His expression was amused. "Who's that? You?"

"Don't look so innocent. Del told me what you called me."

After a startled second, he laughed. "I didn't call you a coward. I've seen you ride. I know you're not a coward. He told me that you said I'd probably say my ma was dead, just so I'd get sympathy if I lost."

"I didn't say that!"

He nodded. "I know you didn't. Now, come on. The road's not far."

For a moment, she thought he'd offer his arm. But that was absurd. He thought she was a boy. Mattie wheeled around and kept pace with him as he strode across the pasture.

When they hit the dusty road, the strong sun soon dried their wet clothes and hair. Within minutes, they were hot again.

"I'm going to light into Del when I see him," Mattie said fiercely.

"He's got his troubles, that boy," Sam said mildly.

"Well, he's about to have more."

A peddler was stopped up ahead, his wagon crammed with goods. Mirrors, pots, toys, fabrics, cheap jewelry. As they came up abreast of the wagon, Mattie caught a flash of color from the bolts of the material. Deep blue, ruby, and one garish calico, pink flowers sprayed against a dull red background.

"You can go on ahead if you want, Matt," Sam said, stopping. "I'll catch up. I need to buy something."

Mattie stopped. It looked as though this peddler had some good items among the cheap bright things placed to catch the eye. Sam didn't seem terribly pleased that she'd lingered, but she didn't care.

It had been so long since she'd seen pretty things.

Mattie eyed a length of striped ribbon. The gold and amber tones would look splendid on Ivy. Mattie had a few coins jingling in her pocket. Buying her sister a present might make up some for worrying her. At least Mattie would like to think so.

Out of the corner of her eye, she saw Sam fingering several bolts of cloth. She noted how his eye went to the finest, the ruby and the dark blue.

"See anything you like? Only got the best." The peddler swung down from the front of the wagon and approached them. He was a bandy-legged, compact fellow with a shiny yellow waistcoat. His checked pants were too tight and stained with grease.

Sam ran his fingers along the ruby stamped velvet. He caught her staring, and one look from his green eyes warned her not to tease him. Mattie quickly looked away.

The ruby velvet was an odd choice for a young man, Mattie thought. He'd have to know a girl fairly well to buy her such a present. He must have a sweetheart, maybe back in Oregon. Was he engaged? She could see by his manner that Sam was embarrassed to have her watching the transaction. It must be a sweetheart, then.

The peddler told him the price, and the two men estimated aloud how much material he'd need. Mattie knew far better than they how much material was needed to make a dress, but she clamped her jaw. No use giving herself away just to help Sam's sweetheart. As a matter of fact, she hoped there wouldn't be enough material, and the girl would end up with a pair of bloomers.

Mattie hated herself for such thoughts. And she was puzzled about where they came from. She didn't even *like* Sam.

She waited while he counted out the money for the expensive material. The peddler kept up a stream of compliments on Sam's taste as he turned his back to wrap the material in brown paper. Sam turned away, embarrassed by the man's flattery.

Mattie put away the ribbon, deciding it wasn't nice enough for Ivy. Opal Pollard back in Last Chance had prettier ribbon than this. She was just in time to see the peddler swiftly replace the velvet cloth with some of the cheap pink flowered calico. In a twinkling, he had wrapped it up in brown paper. By the time Sam unwrapped the package, the peddler would be long gone.

"Hey," Mattie called. "You're not about to cheat my friend, are you?"

The peddler knotted the twine he'd used to

wrap the package. "What are you talking about, young feller?"

"I saw what you just did," Mattie said.

The peddler met her gaze steadily while he pulled out a knife. His small gray eyes locked on hers, beaming a cruel warning. Without dropping his gaze, he cut the twine with the knife. He kept the blade open, watching her.

"Now, you don't want to make trouble, do you, boy?" he said softly. "I wrapped up the fellow's pretty material. You must be mistaken, is all."

The words were a warning, a threat backed up by a knife too razor sharp to be just for cutting twine.

But the peddler didn't know a very important fact about Mattie Nesbitt. She never backed down.

"There's an easy way to settle it," she said steadily. "Open the package."

Sam still hadn't spoken. But she could feel him behind her, waiting. The atmosphere of sudden menace in the air was too sharp to miss.

"I'd like to see myself," Sam said in a bland tone.

The peddler bent over and snapped the twine with the knife. Mattie was relieved when he put the knife down. But it was still in easy reach, glinting on the ledge of the cart.

Her relief vanished as quickly as it came when the

peddler turned back to her and she saw he was holding a revolver. He pointed it straight at her heart.

She stared, fascinated, at the round black hole. It looked like a dead, remorseless eye.

"I think you boys'd better move on," the peddler said. He kept the gun trained on Mattie. "Maybe being young, you ain't aware that you just don't call a man a cheat."

Mattie had lived in California long enough to know that men had been shot for less than a few yards of cloth. But her anger at the peddler was stronger than her fear. Anger that he would try to cheat a young man out of money he'd earned. Sam had sweated for that money, put himself in danger for it, sacrificed for it.

Instead of taking a step back, Mattie stepped forward. She saw the flicker of surprise in the peddler's eyes as she pressed her chest up against the gun. She felt it, hard against her breastbone.

"I said," she repeated steadily, not taking her eyes off him, "you cheated my friend."

The peddler didn't flinch. His eyes were the gray of a cold February day. There was no mercy in them. "You going to die for a half-breed, sonny?" he sneered.

From behind her, Mattie heard the merest

whisper of sound. She saw the peddler's eyes narrow. And then he lowered the gun.

Mattie turned her head. Sam was holding an extremely long knife. He held it loosely, easily, as though it were an extension of his arm. On his face was an expression she'd never seen. In his eyes was a coldness that matched the peddler's and then some. His face was perfectly composed, but she knew that had the peddler made a move, Sam would have cleanly and quietly gutted him like a deer.

With a snarl, the peddler tossed the brown package back into his wagon. He grabbed the ruby velvet and threw it down on the road. Then he swung himself up on the wagon and cracked the whip over his horse. The cart jounced off, tin cups jangling and mirrors shaking.

On legs that trembled, Mattie walked over and picked up the cloth. She dusted it off carefully.

"It's fine," she said. "A little dust won't hurt it."

Sam returned the knife to his boot. There was an odd look on his face as he stared at the dust left by the rapidly moving cart. Mattie couldn't quite interpret it. It was something beyond anger. Something deep and true and cold.

But when he turned to her, the expression was

gone. Mattie read respect in his gaze. It was as clear to her as if he'd spoken it, and a rush of satisfaction flooded her at earning the regard of Sam Brand. She forgot her puzzlement at the coldness she'd seen as she took pleasure in the warmth.

CHAPTER ELEVEN
THE VALLEY OF THE WINDING WATERS

"The cloth is for my mother," Sam explained softly, taking the bundle from Mattie. "I thought it might cheer her to have a new dress."

"It's pretty," Mattie said. "Some black lace would set it off nice."

Sam looked startled. Mattie bit her lip. Darn! She'd sounded just like a girl!

"My sister's a dressmaker," she lied quickly. "She's always going on and on about gowns and such. Some of it rubbed off on me, I reckon."

Sam nodded. He rolled up the material carefully and stuck it under his arm. "Let's sit down for a spell," he said.

He had noted her trembling legs, Mattie knew. She had acted without thinking. Now the fear was pumping through her body, though the danger was over. "I can walk," she said.

"I know," he said. "But let's sit anyway. There's some nice shade over there."

They walked together to a grove of pines. Mattie lowered herself down on the fragrant needles, trying not to sigh with relief.

"Even the bravest man needs to sit down after looking a gun in the face," Sam said easily as he settled himself down. "And my pa told me when you have a brush with death, it's a good idea to get reacquainted with the world again."

Mattie grinned. "Hello, world."

Sam said nothing but sat motionless. Minutes ticked by. Sam seemed content with the silence, but Mattie squirmed with impatience. A question had formed in her mind and she was longing to ask it.

"Why did he call you a half-breed?"

For a moment she was afraid she'd offended him. Sam' squinted at the surrounding hills, the distant mountains.

"'Cause I am one, I expect," he said. "Some folks see it right off. Especially if they've lived out west for a long spell or have traded with Indians. I don't usually tell folks myself. If they think I'm white, I pass."

And she knew, with just a quick sidelong look from Sam's light green eyes, that he had asked her to keep his secret. She also knew that she didn't need to promise him that she would. Not out loud. Sam could ask the favor and exact the promise with just a glance.

The knowledge of Sam's true heritage trickled through her. Mattie didn't have much experience with Indians. She was aware that tribes had lived in the Sierra, and there were still some Indians around Last Chance who eked out a living prospecting. But by and large they avoided the towns. Most of them had been chased off their claims, and they confined themselves to panning for what little was left in mountain streams.

Maybe she should have known, Mattie thought. There had always been an . . . otherness about Sam. A loneliness in his eyes.

"Is your mother Indian?" she asked timidly. Many of the fur trappers, she knew, had taken Indian wives. It was something that had even been encouraged by the fur companies, to tie the men to the West.

Sam nodded. "She's a member of the Nez Perce tribe," he said. "Pa owns a store now, and they've settled up on the Columbia River. I grew up all over the place, though—Pa mostly took us with him when he traveled. But sometimes we'd pass the winter with the tribe. The Nez Perce live in the most beautiful spot on earth. The Valley of the Winding Waters, they call it. The Salmon and Snake Rivers are fast and full of salmon, the meadows are full of flowers, and there's plenty of game to be had in the forests."

"It sounds like the Sierra," Mattie said.

Sam nodded. "It is, only more so. But maybe that's why I feel at home in the Sierra. It's too hard, sometimes, to go back there."

"Why?" Mattie asked curiously.

"The Nez Perce have lived on that land for hundreds of years," Sam said quietly. "In the time of my grandfather's father, the tribe acquired horses, and they became known for their riding skills. They would go in search of buffalo, crossing the great Continental Divide on hunting trips. And when the white man came, they welcomed them. They hosted Lewis and Clark on their great journey, gave them food, and showed them their rivers. There was no hostility to the white man, for the white man had no interest in their land. Not then."

"And now?" Mattie said quietly, afraid to ask.

Sam sighed. He scratched in the dirt with a stick. "There was a council in eighteen fifty-five. The Nez Perce signed a treaty limiting them to a reservation. At least they managed to retain half of their land.

That's better than most tribes were able to achieve. But the prospectors are coming now. And I see what lies ahead. The tribe will soon have to leave the valley. Because with gold seekers come families. With families come towns. And then the U.S. government, making another treaty for it to break."

The wind whispered through the pines above her head. Mattie didn't know what to say. Sam had revealed a whole new way of looking at things. She'd have to struggle to make it fit what she already believed.

She had come west thanks to Eli Bullock's dream of "civilizing" the California frontier. She had believed in his vision of a land with families and churches and laws. She had believed they had come to better the place, to make it finer by pressing it into a civilized mold.

But for the first time, she began to see that this process of civilization was not merely a building thing. It tore down while it built up. A culture lay in dust at their feet, but they simply stamped their boots and went on.

Mattie held those two contrary images in her head and struggled to reconcile them: the building up and the tearing down. People said the Indians didn't matter, that they were savages. But Sam wasn't a savage. She couldn't imagine that his mother was, either. And he described a life that was lived in what seemed to Mattie to be a supremely logical way. To hunt, to fish, to roam—what was wrong with that? And as a Christian, did she have a right to despise it? Folks always said white men were better than the Indians. Was that just because of the way they made their clothes or built their houses or worshiped?

It was all very confusing. She wanted to ask Sam more questions, but he had sunk into a moody silence. She saw that she had, by her question, filled him with sorrow.

Mattie reached out. She was about to touch his sleeve. It was a gesture a woman would make, a gesture of comfort. It would be followed with soothing words, gentle questions.

But she couldn't do any of those things. *Matt* couldn't.

Instead, Mattie pretended to swipe at a fly.

The only thing she could give Sam was her respectful silence. For long moments, she chafed against it. She wanted to speak, to move, to *ask*.

But slowly, the charm of the setting and Sam's quiet breathing calmed her. Mattie's breath came slower, and she matched its rhythm to his.

In her nostrils was the scent of meadow and pine. She noticed with a new clarity how the blue mountains ringed the green valley. The land she loved seemed to rise up around her like a fragrant bowl, cradling her. Mattie felt aware of everything and her place in it.

She was suddenly grateful to Sam for giving her this small gift. Talkative Mattie had learned something. Sometimes silence was eloquence itself.

Now she knew what he'd meant about reacquainting herself with the world around her. She suddenly felt wondrously, powerfully glad to be alive and part of it. *Hello, world*, she said again, but this time the greeting came from her soul.

CHAPTER TWELVE
WHITE WATER

Del had made himself scarce when Mattie and Sam returned, dusty and footsore. Sam borrowed a pony and took off for Placerville, where he was needed to take over his regular route.

"See you on the next run," he said to Mattie.

"You bet," she answered.

"I see the two of you became pals somewhere along the way," Alfie remarked as Sam rode off. "Stranger things have happened, I guess. I won twenty dollars on the race, so I'm not complaining. Had a feeling you'd tie."

"Have you seen Del?" Mattie asked.

Alfie shook his head. "Nursing his wounds, I reckon. He lost a bundle. Probably turn up soon for supper. That boy will always turn up for grub. Which reminds me, I expect you'll be wanting your stew."

"Not really," Mattie murmured under her breath.

But Alfie was already stumping across the porch to the front door.

She went around back to the barn to wait for Del. He'd come by to feed the horses soon, she knew. The sun was sinking over the dark hills, and she hoisted herself up on a fence rail to watch it.

The curve of the sun had disappeared, leaving behind streaks of orange and purple, when Del slinked by in the shadow of the barn.

"Del," she called.

He stopped.

She jumped off the fence and approached him. "Sam and I had a mighty hot walk back," she said conversationally.

Del's eyes darted to the barn. "Is he here?"

He was afraid that the two of them were about to ambush him, Mattie saw. She decided not to correct his impression.

She took a step toward him. "Why are you making trouble for us, Del? We're just trying to do our job, same as you." She took another step.

"I'm not afraid of you, Matt Nesbitt!" Del's voice was shrill. "Or of your new buddy, Sam, neither! You're not better than me just because you ride for the Pony Express!"

"I never said I was," Mattie protested.

"You and Sam go riding off, seeing the country, getting all the men clapping you on the back all the time, and you get to thinking you're as great as they say," Del said, riding over her words. "Throwing me the reins, not even bothering to make conversation over dinner."

"I'm too busy trying to choke down Alfie's stew," Mattie said.

"Don't you sass me!" Del shouted. Even in the dusk, Mattie could see wetness in his eyes. "I'm not your stable boy! I work for the Express, same as you. I could have been a rider. I was too tall. It wasn't because I was fat! That wasn't why!"

Mattie felt taken aback. She didn't know how to react. She was so tired of being a boy! It hemmed a body in so. Because she was a boy, she couldn't acknowledge Del's tears. It would only embarrass him further.

Yet she felt sorry for him. She hadn't realized how much jealousy had fueled Del's actions. She'd taken him at face value, the way she always took people. Since she was direct, she expected other folks to be direct. Ivy always tried to tell her that people weren't always what they seemed.

Ivy would have seen Del's pain. Mattie just saw him as a disagreeable nuisance.

"Del, Sam and I depend on you," she said quietly. "You have a way with horses—"

"Don't you feel sorry for me, neither," Del spat out. He brushed past her so roughly that she stumbled. She hit the trough and teetered. With a precise shove, Del accomplished the rest and pushed her in.

Mattie came up sputtering. Del was already disappearing into the barn. She climbed out of the trough and wrung out the tail of her sodden shirt.

No sense in pursuing it any further, Mattie thought, heading for the station. She couldn't help Del. She couldn't fight him, even though she knew he wanted her to. Wanted "Matt" to.

She'd thought getting a job meant you just got a job. Then you did it. She didn't realize she'd have to get tangled up in other folks' feelings.

She walked inside the station, making puddles on the floor. Mattie headed for the potbellied stove to dry off. Alfie raised a questioning bushy eyebrow at her.

"Something I should know about?"

Mattie shook her head, sending off droplets. "Just needed a bath," she said.

Mattie had been lucky so far. She'd had good weather for all her runs. But on her next one, her luck ran out.

The rain started that night, and it continued all the next day. It drummed on the roof and created a lake in the yard.

Alfie squinted at the sky from the shelter of the porch on the morning she was to ride. "It's not about to let up. You be careful, now. At this time of year, all the streams will be rising."

When Sam arrived, he sent her off with a grim nod. He looked done in, more tired than she'd ever seen him. He must have had a difficult time crossing the mountains.

Mattie galloped off, splashing mud and water. Within seconds, she was wet through. There was nothing for it but to keep going, the cold rain in her face. She was glad when she reached Genoa. In this weather, a fresh mount was essential for keeping her time.

But when she galloped up to the swing station at Carson City, the station tender yelled her on.

"Horse went lame," he shouted in her ear. "You'll have to push on through to Dayton. And be careful of the river, I hear it's rising fast."

Mattie nodded. She spurred her horse and proceeded on. It was bad luck that she couldn't get a fresh horse, but you didn't stop for anything in the Pony Express. You just kept going. Perhaps she would be lucky after all. Perhaps the weather would clear.

But the rain continued to fall, pelting against her face like icy needles. The day grew darker and darker, even though it wasn't close to sunset. The road had become familiar to Mattie, but now she could only see a few feet ahead of her through the curtain of gray rain, making it all look unfamiliar and bleak.

She had to slow her pace a bit because of the rain, even stop altogether once by the side of the road, the downpour was so severe. She was on a good strong gelding, but she knew her mount was tired.

"Just a few miles more, boy," she shouted grimly.

Mattie'd been in the saddle now for eight hours. She was only halfway to her home station. She was worn out, and the river was just ahead.

On a dry, sunny day, crossing the river was accomplished easily. She knew the shallow place to ford, and the horse just splashed through. The only thing she had to watch out for was an occasional snake.

But when she heard the river before she saw it, she knew she was in trouble. Even over the driving rain, she heard the roar. Mattie pulled up a few feet away and squinted through the grayness. Her heart failed her when she saw the boiling river.

The rain had combined with the melting mountain snows to create a torrent. There was no telling how deep it was. Mattie knew she'd have to swim it.

No use waiting. The river would just continue to rise. And there was always the danger of a flash flood, an even deeper sudden rush of water.

Mattie nudged the horse forward. He shied, but with her knees and hands and shouts over the wind she urged him forward. He walked delicately into the churning water. Within a few steps, she could feel the river's pull.

"Come on," she shouted. *"Haw!"* The water rose around her, wild and foaming. It covered her stirrups and receded. It was icy cold.

One more step, and the horse lost his footing. The water was too deep, the current too strong.

"Swim for it, boy!" she shouted, urging him with her knees and hanging on, close to his neck.

But the river seemed to rise and engulf them, and the horse's eyes rolled in fear. She kept a tight rein, but it was no use. They were swept downstream.

"I'm not going to drown," Mattie told herself aloud. Her voice was snatched away by the howling wind. She struggled to keep herself upright. The rain beat against her face, the terrified horse whinnied with its fear, and she hung on, determined to reach the other side. She could just glimpse the opposite bank through the rain. She knew she could make it, she knew she could make it—

They hit a patch of white water. She felt a jolt— perhaps they'd hit a rock. Because suddenly her mount went over, and she was falling into the water, tumbling out of the stirrups, losing the reins, and grabbing for the *mochila,* the most important item she carried.

The shock of the water hit her like a slap.

Mattie felt herself bang against rocks and went down, seeing black river water, seeing death, seeing a blank wall, and she pushed herself up above the surface, gulping air. She found her footing somehow on the slippery rocks, and fighting the pull of the river, she pushed and scrambled, almost falling again, willing herself not to fall, slipping, sliding, half-swimming, she fell again. She felt the crack of the rock against her skull, but she was up again in a moment, pushing on, going on sheer will now, her strength gone. Her feet hit solid ground—the bank. She could only pray it was the opposite one as she hauled herself out of the river. She threw herself down on blessed solid ground, tasting the wet sand with relief. Minus hat, minus horse—but still clutching the leather *mochila* that held the mail.

CHAPTER THIRTEEN
HIGH GROUND

Exhausted and in pain, her face in the dirt, Mattie only knew two things clearly. She had to get to high ground, and she had to find her horse.

She rolled over and winced; she must have banged her shoulder on a rock. She regarded the river. It was rising even as she watched. The rain was falling so hard now that mud splashed up with the impact of the drops hitting the riverbank.

She had landed far downstream, and here the bank of the river was only a few feet wide. Behind her it sloped, then abruptly rose into a low cliff. She could be trapped here if the river overflowed its banks any further.

Mattie had lost her hat, and the rain got in her eyes. She swiped at them and pushed the matted hair off her forehead, slicking it back as best she could. Her hand came back red and was instantly washed off by the rain.

Her head was bleeding. But she didn't have time to worry about it now. Mattie struggled to her feet. Dizziness washed over her as she stood, but she closed her eyes and let out her breath in a sharp hiss, willing it away. When she bent down to retrieve the *mochila*, she almost fell over.

She counted long seconds aloud so that she wouldn't pass out. Then she began to walk. The weight of the *mochila* over her shoulder made her stagger. She slipped and slid on the loose sand and rocks as she made her way downstream. She peered through the rain but saw nothing. If the pony had made it out of the stream, it hadn't been close to where she'd ended up.

Confused thoughts whirled in her head. Should she continue downstream, going further out of her way, or trust that the horse would reach high ground?

Finally she decided to climb to high ground. She'd have a better vantage point if she could see anything through this rain.

The rain had soaked the mixture of dirt and sand, making it almost impossible to get solid footing. There were times when she dropped to her knees and crawled. She was nudging the very end of her strength now, and she knew it.

With a groan of relief, she hauled herself over the

lip of the cliff at last. Her cheek rested against scratchy underbrush. She'd have to push through the tangled branches to find the road.

She stood too quickly. The same sick blankness washed over her brain, and she stumbled and fell.

She woke, her face in the mud. How long had she been passed out—minutes? Hours? It was impossible to tell. The rain still fell in the same drenching downpour.

This time she forced herself to rise gradually, from a sitting position to her knees and to her feet at last. She took another deep breath before she started to walk. Branches slapped against her face and thorns cut her cheeks and hands. She called for her horse, her voice croaking and unfamiliar to her ears.

She was in a spot. Of that she had no doubt. She would be lucky if she could find the road. She was dizzy still, and she kept having to change course slightly to avoid the thick underbrush.

She was now shaking so badly she could barely stumble ahead. Perhaps she should find shelter until morning. But the heaviness of the *mochila* on her shoulder made her press on. If she could only find the road, she would be all right.

Because she wasn't giving up.

She heard a sound. She couldn't place it, but it was different from the rushing wind in her ears, the sound of the rain hammering the ground. And it couldn't be the river—the sound was on her right. Mattie stumbled toward it.

She almost burst into tears when she saw the gray river below. She must have turned around without realizing. She'd been going in the wrong direction, and she couldn't be sure for how long.

Here the river canyon was deeper, and the river was so swollen that it almost reached the steepest sides of the bank. Mattie sent up a silent prayer of thanks that she was safe here, looking down on it.

She had just finished the prayer when the ledge gave way.

Mattie landed on her backside and slid down the slope. The loose, wet mud made a perfect slide, and there was no way she could stop her descent. She grabbed at a branch, she grabbed at rocks, but she kept sliding. She landed back on the riverbank, with the rushing white water only inches away.

Sobbing now, Mattie grabbed the *mochila* from where it had fallen. She was bruised and battered and didn't think her legs could hold her.

The river roared, wild and foaming. The heavy

downpour cleared for just a moment. Mattie saw yards away rather than feet, and what she saw made her heart stop beating.

A wall of water was heading downstream. It must have chunks of the cliff with it, carving out a new channel. She knew that within seconds it would be upon her, and it would sweep her away with the branches and debris, and she would drown if she didn't move—*now*.

She threw herself at the cliff face. It was all rocks and mud, but she hauled herself up, scrabbling and kicking out toeholds. But she wasn't going fast or far enough. . . .

"Matt!"

The voice seemed to come from heaven. But it was above her, and it was Sam.

He threw a rope down to her, and she grabbed it.

He didn't need to say "hang on" or instruct her, because they had only seconds and they both knew what to do.

He hauled. She hoisted. Together they got her above the level of the rushing black river. Though it foamed at her boots and licked angrily at her knees, she was already climbing above it.

With the help of Sam's strength, she reached the top of the cliff. He hauled her up the final inches, and she fell against his legs, her cheek against his boots.

He reached down and picked her up under the arms. He grinned and shook his head when he saw the *mochila*. He took it from her clenched fist.

"The road's a ways," he shouted. "Can you make it?"

She nodded, too exhausted to speak.

He gave her a doubtful look, but he nodded. She started forward and promptly fell down.

Mattie groaned. Her head was spinning so. But she had to get up. She had to walk. . . .

But then strong hands lifted her up by the armpits. She was picked up and cradled against a sodden poncho.

"I got you," Sam said. And he strode on through the rain.

CHAPTER FOURTEEN
WILLING TO RISK DEATH DAILY

She didn't pass out—not quite. But she was lost in a half-world, a cold world of gray shadows. She felt the *thud thud* of Sam's footsteps and the rain trickling down her neck. Every once in a while she would struggle, wanting to walk. But strong arms would tighten against her, and she would have to relax again.

Then they found the road. He sat her on his horse and then got up behind her and took the reins.

Mattie leaned back against Sam. She closed her eyes. She gave up her will and her stubbornness and allowed Sam to bring her to safety. She knew that he would manage. If there was one person she trusted with her life, it was Sam.

She didn't know how long they traveled or how far. She drifted in and out of sleep. But then they were at a cabin, more a ramshackle hut than anything, and Sam was hammering on the door. He put her down on the flat rock that served as a stoop and leaned her gently against the cabin wall. Then he opened the door.

He bent down to pick her up again, but she shook her head. "It's all right," she said faintly. She got herself to her feet by leaning against the wall and sliding up. Then she followed him into the cabin.

It was small and bleak, furnished only with a table and one chair. There wasn't even a bed. Mattie lowered herself into the chair. She began to shake again.

"How did you know about this place?"

"Belongs to a prospector friend of mine," Sam said, looking around. "He usually leaves it stocked with wood and some kind of food."

There was a pile of dry wood in the corner, and Sam soon coaxed a fire out of it despite the wind whistling down the chimney.

"I'll get some coffee going," he said. "There's usually coffee."

Mattie had enough strength to leave the chair and slump closer to the fire. "How'd you find me?"

"Followed your trail," Sam said. "I knew you'd get swept downstream a ways. It wasn't hard to track you, the way you crashed through that brush."

"But why did you come?" The words came out of her with difficulty. Her eyelids were heavy. She desperately wanted to sleep, but just as desperately, she wanted to hear his answer.

"The rain woke me up. I heard Alfie talking to Del about the river. That *really* woke me up. I know this country. I figured you'd be foolish enough to try and swim it. So I decided to make sure you made it." Sam slammed his hand against the wall. Drops flew off his poncho and sprayed against the cabinet. "Where's the blasted coffee? I could skin that old coot alive."

"Why?"

"Because he's always hiding it."

"No, I mean, why'd you come after me?" Mattie had to concentrate to get the words out.

"I just told you," Sam said impatiently. "Look here, Matt. You risked your life just to save me some pennies. Least I could do was check up on you. . . . Ah—coffee. You'd better take off your clothes."

Turning her head away from the fire seemed to take a great effort. "What?"

"Take off your clothes," Sam said, tossing her a blanket. "You'll catch your death if you don't. I'll hang 'em by the fire for you."

Even through the haze, Mattie felt a spurt of panic as her brain struggled with the request. Take off her clothes? Then Sam would know. And even though nothing seemed to have urgency for her now except sleep, she knew that she couldn't let him in on her secret.

He stood impatiently. "Come on, Matt. Do you need me to help you?"

Mattie focused all her energy on meeting Sam's eyes, on looking stronger than she felt. "Nah," she said. She pointed to the leather *mochila* streaming water on the planked floor. "Don't you think you should be going?"

"Going? I can't go and leave you here. You're too weak, Matt."

"I'm all right," Mattie said as forcefully as she could. "I'm just tuckered out, is all. I can make myself coffee, Sam. And keep the fire going. The important thing is to get the mail through."

Sam hesitated.

"Go on," she said impatiently. "I'm already hours behind. You can come back when you get to Fort Churchill, if you want." She plastered a grin on her face. "I'll be sitting here, warm and dry as you please, and feeling fine."

She knew she had him. She was right. She was safe. And the mail had to get through.

"I'll fetch you water first," Sam said reluctantly.

She knew she couldn't argue. She slumped

against the hearth, half-dozing, while he disappeared out back and returned with a jug full of water. "There's a spring out back," he said, putting it on the table. "But this should last you."

"I'm obliged," she said.

"And there's salted beef and crackers in the cabinet."

"Just get going," Mattie said. "Blast your hide."

"I'll be back," Sam muttered. He shouldered the pouches and stomped out.

Mattie kept herself sitting up until the door closed. Then she collapsed on the hearth. The stones were still cold. The fire hadn't had a chance to warm them.

Moving slowly, resting every minute or so, Mattie managed to strip off her boots and wet clothes. She left them in a sodden heap and drew the blanket he'd tossed to her over herself.

There was more wood to get. The fire wouldn't last long. And the thought of hot coffee warming her belly made her moan with want. She was so cold. But she knew she didn't have the strength to make it.

What she needed was sleep. Then she would be able to rise, build up the fire, make coffee, find food. She was shaking uncontrollably now, and her skin felt clammy and cold. She turned her face to the fire and told herself sleep would come.

When she woke, the fire was out. It was cold in the cabin. The rain was still drumming on the roof, and a draft blew down the chimney. Mattie looked at the blanket and saw she was covered with ash.

If her skin had felt cold before, now it was hot to the touch. Yet she was freezing. Mattie groaned.

"I must get up," she said aloud. The sound of her voice frightened her. It was so weak.

She longed for her sister's cool hands on her forehead. If only Ivy were here to spoon broth in her mouth, bring her weak tea, sit by her bed, and sponge her hot skin with cool cloths!

Inside her, a voice scolded her in disgust. She couldn't ride for eight hours, swim a raging river, and lie helpless on a cabin floor! She wasn't a weakling.

Mattie tried to rise, but her head swam, and she felt sick. She fell back on the hearth. The chair across the floor seemed to float in front of her eyes.

More rest, she thought woozily. Just a little more rest, and she'd be able to get up.

CHAPTER FIFTEEN
A NIGHT BY THE FIRE

"Blast!"

The word penetrated Mattie's foggy sleep. Loud thumps resounded through the cabin. She struggled to open her eyes.

A wet and furious Sam was stomping through the cabin. The bones of his face stood out, the skin stretched tightly over them. He must be exhausted, Mattie thought dizzily.

She watched through glazed eyes as he threw wood in the fireplace and kindled a fire. She could see how he fought his impatience, wrestled and controlled it, in order to get the deed done.

A friendly blaze roared up the chimney. Sam disappeared and came back with a bundle wrapped in a tarp. He unwrapped the package and disclosed a thick quilt. He tucked it around her.

"Did you eat anything?" he asked. His voice was rough, but she could see the worry in his green eyes.

He sucked in air through his teeth. "Don't bother to answer, I can see you didn't. Hang on, Matt."

He kept up a steady stream of curses as he unwrapped his pack. He dumped something in a pot and hung it over the fire. Then he ground coffee and hung the coffeepot over the fire as well. Still cursing, he stripped off his wet poncho and then down to his long underwear.

She should have felt the warmth from the fire and the quilt, but she didn't. Mattie wondered if she was too cold ever to be warm again.

Sam stamped over to her. To her surprise, he lay himself down next to her and put his arms around her.

Mattie stiffened.

"Now, don't go getting all het up," Sam said irritably. "It's the only way to get you warm. He rubbed his hands down her arms. "You're nothing but skin and bones, Matt. No wonder you caught such a chill."

Slowly Mattie relaxed. The thick quilt was between their bodies. There was no way that Sam could discover her sex. But underneath the blanket and quilt, she was naked. Her clothes were still in a heap in front of the fire and were probably damp. Sooner or later she would have to get up.

But she didn't worry about that now. It was enough to have Sam take care of her and to know that she was safe.

"I shouldn't have left you, Matt. I should have seen how you weren't able to take care of yourself. I thought you were better than you were. And I also thought that Phineas—that's my friend who lives here—would get here before I returned. That the storm would drive him inside. But he must be holed up somewhere, waiting it out. I thought a lot of things. None of them were true."

He spoke while he rubbed her vigorously with his strong hands. Finally warmth did begin to creep inside Mattie's body. She felt the heat of the fire on her face and the delicious thick warmth of the quilt.

"That feels better, Sam," she said. "I'm better already."

"No, you're not," Sam replied calmly. "I felt your skin before; you've got a fever. But I don't expect you're going to die."

"Glad to hear it," she said.

"I'll see to the soup." He sprang up and looked into the pot. "I hear Charley Goodnight isn't a half-bad chef. I brought his stew."

"He isn't as bad a cook as Alfie," Mattie said weakly. "But dang it all, he keeps trying."

Sam laughed. He used the cuff of his shirt to protect his hands against the hot handle of the iron pot. He poured the soup into a bowl and brought it to her with a battered spoon.

He had to feed her the soup. Mattie kept her bare arms underneath the blanket. She shook her head after a few spoonfuls, but Sam insisted on feeding her the whole bowl. As soon as she'd finished, Mattie felt sleepy again.

"You go ahead and sleep now," Sam said. "That's what you need. I'll keep the fire going."

"You need sleep, too," Mattie said drowsily.

"Don't you worry about me right now," he said. His voice was kind. "Just be quiet. Go to sleep, Matt."

And for once Mattie did what she was told.

She awoke drenched in sweat. The fever had broken. That was good. She was on the mend. Ivy always said that Mattie had a constitution of iron.

She looked across the hearth. Wrapped in a blanket, Sam slept heavily. The fire had burned down, but the embers burned orange, surrounded by white ash.

Mattie stripped off the quilt and the blanket and rose on legs that wobbled. Sam had left her clothes draped over the chair, and they were completely dry now. She wiped off the perspiration on her body with her shirt. Now it was almost as wet as it had been in the storm. She slipped into Sam's. It hung to her knees and smelled of sweat and horse and Sam.

Clutching at the table to keep her balance, she got wood from the pile and added it to the fire. It blazed up again, its orange light flickering on Sam's lean face. He didn't wake.

She sank down on the hearth to look at him. With sleep the creases of fatigue had smoothed out. He had been in the saddle for over twenty hours, by her reckoning. He had ridden through a rainstorm to save her, then had taken the mail to Fort Churchill, turned around, and come back for her.

In the firelight he looked younger. She realized that the usual impassive mask he wore was fashioned as much from defensiveness as detachment. She saw a vulnerability to his mouth and a softness to his features she didn't notice when he was awake.

Her hand moved forward as though she hadn't directed it. She touched his cheek, the barest whisper of contact. He didn't stir.

She knew this kind of rest, the sleep of pure exhaustion. He wouldn't wake.

Her hand moved to his thick, straight hair. She smoothed it off his forehead. It was a strange sensation, to feel his hair, the shape of his head. Intimate and yet familiar. As though she had stroked him before in her dreams.

No, not her dreams, Mattie corrected. Someplace even deeper than dreams.

Because she knew him, inside and out. She knew him without spending even a hundred hours in his presence. She knew how his pride kept his spine straight and his face aloof. She knew his humor and his tenderness. She thought she even knew the dreams that drove him.

It had happened just the way Ivy had said it would. Ivy had struggled to describe the way she'd fallen in love with Justus. "It happened so slowly—and then so fast," she'd told Mattie finally, helplessly.

Mattie had noticed Sam. Something about him drew her to him. But he'd pricked her pride, irritated her, stung her, ignored her, and she'd decided she didn't care about him at all. But all the while she'd been thinking of him.

She pitted herself against him, and they'd come out even. And when they'd become friends, she'd felt cheered, thinking that it was what she'd wanted all along.

But now she knew that she felt more for Sam than just friendship. From now on, no matter if she was near him or on the other side of a mountain range, he would be central in her life. She would be his, right down to the bone.

This small corner of the earth had changed because he walked upon it.

She reached out and touched his cheek again. She felt the living warmth of him, the particular feel of his skin, the mark of his scent.

She loved him. And because of that one great, enormous fact, she knew that her problems were just beginning.

CHAPTER SIXTEEN
BOOTS AND PANTS

Two things were between her and Sam. Namely, boots and pants.

He knew her as Matt. A comrade, a fellow he competed with and maybe felt a little protective toward. Like a younger brother, perhaps. He had grown to respect her, even like her a little bit.

But not as a girl.

Suddenly Mattie felt cold. She returned to her makeshift bed and tunneled under the blanket and quilt. Her face toward the fire, she pondered her predicament.

Could she tell Sam she was a girl? Just come out with it? And if she did, would she lose her job? Was she willing to risk that? Or should she wait until her two months were up and then tell him?

But would he hate her for deceiving him? Sam was honest to the bone.

Mattie sighed. Even if she did find the right way

and the right time to tell him, even if he did forgive her, it still wouldn't matter. Because she wasn't the kind of girl he wanted. She knew that. In his eyes, she was a girl too plain to matter. She was a wallflower.

And if she couldn't stand to see disgust in his eyes, indifference would be worse.

With that last, despairing thought, Mattie drifted off to sleep.

Sam had already built up the fire when she awoke. Barechested, looking healthy and rested, he had already tidied up his bedroll and started coffee. He had been out and had replenished the woodpile.

"'Morning," he said when he saw she was awake. "The storm's over, but the river's still too high to cross. And I met a traveler on the road. He found your horse. Seemed a mite put out that he wasn't going to get to keep him. I tethered him out back."

"That's good news," she said, sitting up.

"That's not all," he said, grinning. "I bought some bread and bacon off him."

"Even better," she said. "I'm hungry."

"You look better."

"The fever broke last night," Mattie said, stretching. Quickly, she lowered her arms again.

She forgot that she was wearing only Sam's shirt.

But he hadn't noticed her figure. His grin grew wider. "See you found a clean shirt."

"It isn't so clean," she shot back.

Smiling, he turned back to slice the bacon. Mattie sprang up quickly. It caused her head to spin, but she grabbed at her trousers and pulled them on.

Sam put out plates on the hearthstones. They ate their breakfast cross-legged in front of the fire, spearing bacon from the pan between them.

"It'll take a day or so to get your strength back," Sam advised. "Best to take it easy. You rest today."

"Alfie will have my hide if I'm not back," Mattie said, chewing.

"Alfie's more gurgle than guts," Sam said. "And anyway, he'll know the river's too high to cross yet. Speaking of Friday's Station, though, I've got another piece of news. I was saving it until you were feeling better. Del asked to get transferred. So he won't be bothering you anymore. I heard about the horse trough."

"He wasn't so bad," Mattie said.

"There's a spot open in the Carson City station. He's still on your route, but at least it's just a swing station. You won't see much of him."

"I wonder why he left," she said.

"I think he wants to prove himself to Alfie," Sam said, checking the coffee. Finding it was done, he poured out two cups.

Mattie speared another slice of bacon from the pan. "Why? He didn't even like him."

"Didn't you know? Del is Alfie's son."

The bacon stopped halfway to Mattie's mouth. "He is? But they never said anything."

"Well, it's one of those things everybody knows but nobody talks about," Sam said. "Alfie never admitted he was Del's father. Del's mother is a waitress in Virginia City. Maybe Alfie would have married her, but he's married already to someone back east."

"Sounds like a sad story."

Sam shrugged. "I guess Del thought since Alfie got him the job, he was ready to acknowledge him. But Alfie just kept needling him. I felt sorry for Del. That's why I never rode him about leaving us stranded at the lake."

Mattie took a sip of coffee. "I feel awfully stupid I didn't see it."

"No reason you should," Sam said with a shrug. "I just guessed because of them looking so much alike. Something behind the eyes that's the same. And of course there was the sting in Alfie's needling that gave it away, too. Then on my way back from

Oregon, I heard folks talk about it in Virginia City. Have the last piece of bacon, Matt."

Mattie broke the bacon in two and put half on Sam's plate. She'd never noticed anything amiss between Alfie and Del. When was she going to learn how to really look into folks, instead of right at them?

It felt good to be sitting up, gossiping with Sam. She tore off a hunk of bread and wrapped it around the piece of hot bacon. One of the many good things about being a boy was that you could eat when you were hungry. You could talk with your mouth full, too. She didn't have to nibble daintily at a corner of the bread when she wanted a nice big mouthful.

Then Mattie remembered how Jenny Scarborough picked at her food, and her hand stopped halfway to her mouth. Here she was cramming food into herself, not thinking about the day when Sam would know who she really was. He would remember how she really ate and scratched and cussed, and he would have to conclude that underneath her white dress she was no lady.

"Feeling poorly again?" Sam asked.

Mattie put down the bread. "Just resting."

"Just goes to show what happens when you live a lie," Sam remarked.

Mattie choked on her coffee. "What?"

"Del and Alfie," Sam said. "Nobody ends up winning, do they. Are you all right, Matt?"

"Fine," she croaked.

He reached for another hunk of bread. "You're nothing but a runt, aren't you. Somebody's got to look out for you."

She heard the fondness behind his gruff words, and her heart gave a tiny leap. You couldn't just push liking out of your heart, could you? Just for the sake of one tiny lie?

She picked up the bread again, her appetite back. "Why don't you want anybody to know you're half-Indian, Sam?" she asked, biting into it.

He took a long sip of coffee and put the mug back down on the hearthstone. His mouth twisted in a way that made her heart hurt.

"The Nez Perce have never attacked a white man," he said. "But folks tend to lump all Indians into one category—savages."

"Not all folks," Mattie said.

"*Most* folks," Sam said gently. "I know there are exceptions, Matt. Like my pa. But I have firsthand knowledge of how the white man treats Indians. And I've seen savagery from white men that makes Indians look docile."

He half-stood to poke at the fire, then sat down again. "It's hard to explain to a full-blood white, Matt," he said, brooding. "If the Express knew I was half-Indian, things would be different. I could get fired straight out, first of all. But if I stayed, well, say I was late on a run or lost a letter. They'd say, he's a no-account Indian, you know. Everything I did or didn't do would be judged by that one thing."

Mattie didn't say anything. She thought he was exaggerating, but she didn't want to say so. After all, he'd already been riding for the Express for months. She couldn't see why they'd judge him differently just because his mother was an Indian.

"Shucks," Sam said. "It's the little things, too. At that fair in Grass Valley, for example, I couldn't even ask a pretty girl to dance, wondering if she'd look at me and call me a half-breed. I was never comfortable in the white world for that reason, always wondering who would turn away. I never even learned to dance like a white man. What was the use?"

So that was why Sam had been so awkward on the dance floor! That was why he'd held her so stiffly, rocking back and forth like a ship! He hadn't known any better. Maybe that was the reason he was so reluctant when Justus forced him on her!

Mattie stood and dusted the crumbs off her

trousers. "I'll teach you," she said. "Come on. My sister taught me."

He looked up at her skeptically. "Now?"

"Now."

"There's no music."

"We don't need music."

"Have you been eating loco weed? I'm not dancing."

She laughed and tugged at his arm. "Come on. Nobody will see. And the next time you're at a fair, you can ask a girl to dance." *And I hope it will be me.*

Sam rose to his feet, his face full of reluctance. Mattie began to hum.

"Move your feet like this," she directed, and he followed clumsily.

"Just follow along," Mattie urged, humming. He stumbled through the steps in his heavy boots, trying to follow her stockinged feet.

He laughed. "I'm an awful puddin' foot."

"You're doing fine," Mattie said, laughing along with him.

When he was following her steps more gracefully, she took his hand and put it around her waist.

"Now, this is how you hold the girl," she said. "One hand around the waist, like that. And one hand here." She took his hand in hers.

Sam stopped smiling. Their faces were very close. Some emotion moved behind his eyes, something she couldn't place. She could feel his confusion, the way his hand trembled at her waist. The moment spun out into a span of time impossible to measure, impossible to stand.

Sam dropped his hands and stumbled backward. She saw him swallow.

"Sam—," she said.

He turned away with a groan. He knew something was amiss, but he didn't know what. Mattie reached out and touched his bare shoulder, and he flinched.

"Sam," she said firmly. "Look at me."

He turned back. She smiled, a real smile, Mattie's smile, not Matt's grin. It was the smile of a woman, and Sam froze, staring at her.

She took a deep breath. "How do you do, Sam," she said, sticking out her hand. "I'm Mattie."

CHAPTER SEVENTEEN
FIRE AND SMOKE

Sam's brain whirled. He took a step backward. The face before him was familiar, yet not. Suddenly the bright blue eyes were . . . different. The light in them was warm, seductive. The body he'd thought of wiry was now slender. He could almost imagine the curves. . . .

Matt was . . . Mattie. A girl. A woman.

And then the knowledge roared through his brain. She was the girl he'd danced with at the fair! The girl he'd been too embarrassed to talk to. The girl he couldn't wait to get away from . . .

"Mattie," he said.

She dropped her hand. "I did it so I could ride," she said faintly.

He'd always known there was something different about Matt. He'd—she'd—had a gentler way about her than most fellows.

"I guess I fooled you too well," she said. Her voice

was soft, tentative. "You look about to keel over."

"That day I bought the dress material," he said, remembering. "You said how to trim the dress. It wasn't something a fellow would say."

"But you didn't know," she said.

"No," he said. "I didn't know." Because Matt had pressed his chest up against a gun barrel, and he'd never doubted he was male.

Funny, though, how he'd felt strangely protective of Matt. The boy was no smaller or skinnier than some of the other riders. But there was something about him that invited Sam's care. Sam hadn't wondered about it, just accepted it. Sometimes you just felt peculiar connections to people without knowing quite why.

But he'd been wrong all along. It wasn't a connection. It was a nagging feeling that something was wrong, off.

"Sam?" Matt—Mattie's voice was softer now, a bit higher. A girl's voice. "Are you mad?"

"I've been competing with a girl," he said, shaking his head. "Folks bet on my racing against a *girl*. And I didn't even win!"

"What difference does that make?" Mattie asked, her eyes wide.

He paced around the cabin. He was full of a

pent-up emotion—anger, shame—he couldn't put a name to it. It spilled over, messy and familiar. He was always wary of being mocked, and now he'd been mocked without his realizing. He'd been trading insults and challenges with a *girl*! Folks had set him up to tie with a *girl* as the fastest Express rider!

"Sam, will you settle down?" Mattie said. "You're going to shake the whole cabin to smithereens if you keep stomping around like that."

He whirled around to face her. "You *lied*!" he flung at her. "Are you so ashamed to be who you are?"

"I'm not ashamed!" Mattie said hotly. "It's not my fault that the world thinks a girl can't do things a man does! That scout asked me to join the Express before he knew I was a girl. Then as soon as he found out he just laughed at me. Is that fair?"

"Is it fair to lie to people?" he countered. "Just because you have a silly whim and want to prove you're just as tough as the boys?"

"It's not a whim," Mattie said furiously.

"And putting yourself in danger with your foolishness," he said. "You could have been drowned that night on the river; do you know that?"

"That's not fair, Sam," she said. "I could have drowned as a boy as well as a girl. What difference does it make?"

"It makes a big difference," he said meaningfully.

Mattie stamped her foot. "How dare you," she shouted. "How dare you say it happened because I was a girl! You didn't think so when I was Matt! You're just saying that because your pride's hurt. And that's a pretty rotten reason to be mean!"

Sam's mouth worked. He wanted to blast her with angry words. He wanted to open the top of her head and pour sense in it. He wanted to grab her and shake her.

Instead, he grabbed the shirt hanging over the chair and put it on. It was hers, he realized. He'd have liked to fling it off angrily, but then she was wearing *his* shirt, and things could get complicated.

"I'm going to check on the river," he said.

The door banged shut behind him. Mattie did something she hadn't done since she'd become a boy. Something she rarely did as a girl. She burst into tears.

Sam was gone most of the day. He returned at dusk, his saddlebags bulging with food. He dumped them on the table without a word.

"Phineas is prospecting on the Feather River," he said shortly. "Won't be back for weeks. River is still high. I brought dinner."

He didn't ask her how she was feeling or how she'd spent the day. Just as well, Mattie reflected, chin in hand, staring at the fire. She'd spent it wondering about him. It had been a beastly day.

But she had slept through the afternoon, and she could feel her strength returning. Sam had shot a couple of rabbits, keeping one and trading the other for carrots and greens for a stew. He'd also obtained a bit of sugar for their coffee. It was a good dinner.

But it was agony. He didn't speak. He ate. Mattie pushed her food around her plate. She discovered that she was a girl, after all. When faced with emotional turmoil, she lost her appetite. At least she was demonstrating ladylike behavior. Maybe Sam would find that appealing.

"You're not going to get better, eating like a bird," he said in disgust as he cleared the plates.

She couldn't win. And now dinner was over, and night had fallen, and there were long hours to get through. Tension hung in the cabin, thick and heavy. They had spent the night under the same roof before. But tonight was different.

"I'm going to turn in," Sam said. "I suggest you do the same."

His words hung in the air. He started to unbutton his trousers and stopped. He rolled himself in the blanket fully clothed and turned his back to her.

Mattie stayed dressed as well. She crawled under the quilt. She lay on her back and stared at the sagging ceiling. The wood in the fire snapped.

She had to force herself to lie still. She was filled with an uncomfortable, restless energy. She wanted to jump up and pace. She wanted to ride her horse until they were both in a lather. She wanted . . .

She wanted to sleep next to Sam and feel his body pressed against hers.

Shocked at herself, Mattie squirmed. But she had seen so much of Sam. She had traced the outlines of his face with light fingers. She had followed the contours of muscle and bone in his chest with her eyes. She had noted the way the brown skin of his back glistened, how there was a triangle of light hairs at the small of his back where it disappeared into his trousers.

She had thought Justus and Ivy silly, with their traded glances and the way they would touch fingers when they thought nobody was looking. Now she understood their longing.

She turned on her side. Sam was just a lump in a blanket, but she could just trace the outline of a thigh, the curve of a hip. Was he lying awake, just as she was, burning with the possibility that existed between them? All one of them had to do was cross the few hearthstones and begin with the first touch. All the angry words would dissolve in the sweet pleasure of a kiss.

She wished he would turn. She wished his eyes would open. She wished his gaze would turn smoky when it rested on her. She remembered the way his hand had trembled when it rested on her waist. Somewhere inside he'd known. He'd felt his attraction. It had confused him. But it was there. Was it beating a pulse inside him, as steady and sure as hers?

She had never had a problem being bold. Why was she so afraid now?

It was the hardest thing she'd ever done. Lying rigid, she gathered her courage. She told herself that to be strong, she had to yield.

"Sam?" she whispered.

He should be happy. After all, she had been the one to surrender. He didn't have to lie awake with longings, with questions. He only had to turn.

"Sam?" she spoke the word louder.

She was answered with a soft snore. He wasn't awake. He wasn't burning. He wasn't even mildly piqued.

He was asleep.

CHAPTER EIGHTEEN
A SIMPLE FEMININE LONGING

She woke to the sound of Sam's boots thudding against the floorboards. She blinked sleepily at him.

"I'm going to check on the river again. It should be down by now. We can leave this morning."

She nodded. Her eyes were wide with expectancy. But for what, she didn't know.

"Just stay put," he said in a grudging tone. "You're still too weak to get about alone."

"But I'm better—"

"Don't argue," he said tersely. "You'll be a heap more trouble to me if you get sick again. There's coffee and bread for breakfast."

He walked out.

Furious, Mattie flung off the blanket. She poured a cup of coffee and burned her mouth on it.

She yanked open the cabin door and looked out at a green and fragrant world. There was a strong hot sun in the clear blue sky. Mattie leaned against the door frame with her coffee. It had been days and days since she'd seen the sun.

And with the sun and her renewed strength she looked down at herself for the first time. Her clothes were filthy. Sam's shirt was stained from his ride, and her pants had dried stiff with mud. She touched her hair. It felt rough and matted.

She needed a bath.

It was a simple feminine longing. To be clean, to be fresh. To once again have silky hair and skin that wasn't salty from perspiration. As long as she was officially a girl again, couldn't she indulge the desire? Sam wouldn't be back for hours yet.

She left her empty cup on the table and searched for soap, finally finding one thin cake wrapped in a rag at the back of the cabinet. Obviously, Phineas wasn't much for bathing.

Taking the cake of soap, she headed out in search of the source of the springwater Sam pumped for them each morning. She heard the sound of running water and found the stream down a small hill. She followed it until it emptied into a pool. Perfect.

Mattie stripped and slid into the water. The shock of the cold made her shiver, but the fresh feeling against her skin was worth the chill. She soaped her arms and chest and went to work on her hair.

It felt marvelous to feel the sweat and dirt slide off her body. Mattie ducked underneath the cool fragrant water and let it run through her short hair.

Before she could get a chill, she hoisted herself up on the grassy bank. The sun felt good on her cool skin. She felt so fresh that she couldn't bear to put on her dirt-encrusted clothes. But she was afraid they wouldn't have a chance to dry if she washed them. Sam would be furious if she only had wet clothes to wear for their journey back.

Mattie closed her eyes and tilted her head back to receive more of the sun's rays. She tucked her knees up to her chest to shield herself. Sam had told her that they were well off the road, but you never knew when a stray traveler would happen by. She kept her shirt within easy reach.

"What the devil do you think you're doing?"

The harsh voice frightened her. Her eyes flew open even as she grabbed for the shirt.

She hadn't recognized the voice, but it was Sam. He stood on the opposite bank, hands on his hips.

Keeping herself shielded as best she could, Mattie slipped into her shirt.

"I was taking a bath," she called over the water. "And looking for some privacy to do it in, I might add."

"Are you crazy?"

Making an impatient movement, Sam strode down the bank and disappeared past the trees. She knew he was looking for a place to cross.

Within moments, he was standing over her, blocking out the sun.

"You just got over being sick!" he shouted.

"Don't shout at me!" she yelled.

"I'm not shouting!" he roared. He tore off his jacket and threw it over her shoulders. "You have the sense of a chicken! You're still weak, Mattie!"

She stood, clutching the jacket. "Stop treating me like . . . like a girl!" she sputtered.

"I'm treating you like a girl because you are," he said to her patiently, as though she were a child. His tone was a match lighting a fuse of dynamite.

Mattie hauled off and pushed him as hard as she could. Sam stumbled, catching himself before he fell.

"What in tarnation are you doing?" he bawled.

"I wasn't so *weak* just then, was I?" she taunted. She sprang forward and shoved him again. Harder. He staggered back against a boulder, and his feet got tangled up. With a startled *oof,* Sam went down.

She stood over him, her hands on her hips. "I said I was a girl," she said sweetly. "I never said I was a lady."

"That's for certain," he said, rubbing his backside. He stood up wearily. "I don't want to fight with you, Mattie. I don't think my body could stand it."

"I don't want to fight, either," Mattie said. "But I will, if you keep treating me different like you are. Go ahead, be mad at me for deceiving you and everybody. I can stand that. But I *can't* stand your treating me like I all of a sudden turned into a week-old kitten. I'm the same person who almost beat you in a horse race—twice. I'm the same person who rides for the Pony Express. I have the same brain, the same heart. Why can't you treat me the same?" she demanded.

"You're not the same!" Sam thundered in exasperation. "You're . . . *soft*!" He spit the word out in disgust.

"I'm not soft," she argued hotly. "I'm just as tough as I ever was!"

Mattie saw Sam's mood change as swiftly as clouds passing across a rock face. He reached out and touched the skin of her forearm. His finger ran over the veins at her wrist. "I mean soft this way," he said quietly.

The breath left Mattie's body in a whoosh. "Oh," she managed.

Sam kept his warm fingers on her cool skin.

"When I saw you on the bank, my heart stopped."

Mattie swallowed. "Why?" she whispered.

His fingers ran up underneath the unbuttoned cuff of her shirt. She shivered as she felt them brush against her skin. "Because I knew how soft you'd be," he said. "I knew it last night, too, seeing your skin in the firelight, the way it lit up your eyes and your hair. I couldn't sleep a wink."

"Liar," she said mockingly. "You snored."

"I was only pretending," Sam said.

Joy rose in Mattie's heart. "You were?"

"It was dangerous," he said. He took a step closer to her. "To be lying next to you like that. I couldn't breathe. For the first time in my life, I was afraid, Mattie."

"Afraid of what?" she whispered, hardly daring to ask.

"Afraid I'd do this," he said. And then his mouth descended on hers.

CHAPTER NINETEEN
KISSES CAN BE DANGEROUS

First slowly, then fast.

This was the fast part.

Pure sensation flooded her. Her reliable brain let her down. She was all rushing, spinning feeling.

The kiss was tentative. His mouth was cool and smooth. But she'd known, somewhere, somehow, it would be. She'd known how perfectly it would fit on hers.

They stood, mouths together. Sam's hands explored her arms, shoulders, hair. His legs were slightly spread apart, and she was nestled between them. She'd thought they were near to the same size, but Sam was bigger up close. His body felt harder and stronger than she'd thought, too. It seemed perfectly designed to hold her there, against him.

When the kiss deepened, Mattie's legs buckled. She'd never been kissed like this. In Maine, snatched kisses in an orchard from a childhood playmate. In Last Chance, a swiftly grabbed kiss from a courting miner on her porch one night. None of them had compared to this.

This was like being in the raging, swollen river, swept downstream despite her efforts.

Still clinging to each other, they fell to their knees. Sam bent her backward onto the grass, his sinewy body covering hers. She sighed into his mouth, and he gripped her tighter.

Funny how she'd traveled halfway around the world to find home. Because Sam *was* home. With the sun overhead and the smell of spring in her nostrils, she felt a part of earth and sky. She felt she was smack in the center of the world, right where she belonged.

Sam lifted his head. A slow, drowsy smile spread over his face. A new smile, Mattie noted with happiness; one she'd never seen before. She liked it.

He rubbed his hands along her rough, shorn hair. He traced the freckles on her nose. He examined her seriously now, his eyes grave, from her earlobes to her collarbone. He even picked up her wrist to trace the fine, delicate bones there.

"Yup," he said slowly, "you're a girl, all right."

With a twist of his lithe body, he flipped over to

his back on the grass next to her. For a moment, she just listened to his breathing.

"Mattie, you've got me so confused I feel like I'm walking backward," he said finally.

She chuckled. "I know how you feel."

"Maybe we can sort it out when we get back across the river. When you're wearing a dress again."

The sun must have darted behind a cloud, because a shadow fell on the bright morning.

"What do you mean?" Mattie asked.

"When you give up the Express," he said.

Mattie paused. She knew this was an important moment, but it was not one she relished. She drew her shirt closer around her bare legs.

"I'm not giving up the Express, Sam."

She heard his breath go out, then in. "I thought that was a given, Mattie."

"Why?"

He sounded impatient now. "We've talked about this. You know how dangerous it can be."

"I always knew how dangerous it could be," Mattie countered. "That's hardly a reason. Unless you tell on me and I get fired. *That* would be a reason."

"I'm not going to tell on you," Sam said testily. "You know that. But I did catch you in a lie. It's up to you what to do about it."

Up till now they had been lying quietly, side by side, staring up at the sky. Now Mattie shot to a sitting position, her muscles rigid with indignation.

"And what about you, Sam Brand?" she demanded. "You're living a lie, same as me. You're afraid to tell them you have Indian blood in you!"

"That's not the same!" Sam exclaimed, sitting up.

"It's exactly the same," Mattie argued. "We're fighting the same battle. We'll both be judged on something that has nothing to do with whether we can be trusted to do the job."

"Mattie, I have good reason for my decision," Sam said with infuriating calm. "It's not based on vanity."

"*Vanity!*" she sputtered.

He didn't answer, just continued looking at her with green eyes clear as a mountain pool.

Strange how love could turn, just like that, Mattie thought. A moment ago she'd loved him so much her heart was full to bursting. Now she hated him more than she'd ever hated anyone in her life.

Her eyes narrowed. "I have good reason, Sam. It's not based on something that might be. It's based on something that is."

His face was stony, closed to her. "What does that mean?"

"You're thinking they'll treat you differently

once they know. But you're thinking that out of bitterness. You're like a dog who had a bad master and was always getting kicked. Even though you're in a new household, you're still cringing, waiting for the blow."

"You're calling me a *dog*?" he roared, springing to his feet. "You're saying I'm *cringing*?"

She leaped up to face him. "Don't get all riled up," she said scornfully. "What I'm saying is that you're a *man*. You're in that particular confederacy. You've ridden and shot and proved yourself. And you'll go on riding and shooting and doing whatever blame-fool thing you want. Because you *can*. Because you're a man. If you want to keep riding for the Express, you can. If you want to quit and buy land, you can. So stop bellyaching!"

"Bellyaching," he repeated. He stared at her as though she were a plant that he'd realized was poisonous after he'd swallowed a big mouthful.

"This is my one chance," she said. "It's not yours. You have plenty of chances. That's all."

Mattie felt sure of herself, and proud, and strong. But then the argument, the heat, and the empty stomach suddenly introduced themselves to her weakened body. All her blood seemed to drain out of her, and she weaved.

Sam caught her as she fell. The grimace on his face told her that she'd just lost her argument. She'd succumbed to feminine behavior by swooning.

She'd never swooned in her life. It was all very confusing, but she knew one thing for sure: It was all Sam's fault.

He lowered her onto the grass. "Put your head between your knees," he instructed gruffly.

Mattie took several gulps of air. Perspiration prickled the back of her neck. She should have eaten breakfast instead of just having that coffee. She should have splashed in the pond instead of immersing herself.

And she never should have kissed Sam Brand.

She lifted her head. "I'm better now."

"Sure," Sam said tersely. "Well, that decides it. You're not fit to ride, and I can't stay with you any longer."

"I can rest at Friday's Station—"

He snorted. "With Alfie's cooking? You'll be dead in a week."

Sam picked up his hat and put it on. A shadow fell over his eyes. "Here's what's going to happen. I'm putting you on the stage at Carson City. You're going home to your sister. And if you so much as say one word, I *will* tell on you."

CHAPTER TWENTY
LAST CHANCE

Numb with fatigue and distress, Mattie didn't bother to argue with Sam. She wasn't foolhardy. She knew she needed a few more days' rest before taking on the rigors of the Express route.

So it was that knowledge more than Sam's threat that caused her to board the stage at Carson City without a word of protest.

As for Sam, well. He hadn't said much on the ride to the stage. He hadn't said much as they bought her ticket. He hadn't said much as they waited for the stage, and he hadn't said much as he helped her to board.

And to top off all of that dazzling eloquence, as the stage began to move, he'd come out with "Good-bye."

Stages were built and run solely for speed, not comfort. Mattie had never ridden in one before, preferring her own transportation or the homely wagon of Willie Joe Franklin, who had a regular run hauling freight from Last Chance to Sacramento and San Francisco.

She found herself wedged into the small compartment with nine other passengers. Her back was to the horses, and her knees had to interlock with the person's opposite her. Because of the mail and luggage tied onto the boot of the coach, she and the other passengers on her bench were constantly pitched forward. It was hard to keep her balance as the coach jounced its way over the mountain roads.

A steady wind whistled through the coach, bringing clouds of dust. By the time they'd reached Genoa, half the male passengers had lost their hats. Mattie had sat on her own hat in order to preserve it, and dust grains constantly flew into her streaming eyes.

There had been reports of Paiutes being particularly "unfriendly," and nerves were strung tight among the passengers. Every unusual jolt of the stage caused a lady who had been traveling all the way from St. Joseph, Missouri, to scream "Indians!" until Mattie had cause to regret not having her revolver handy.

Sam had wanted to save her strength by sending

her home by stage. He just might have killed her. Her fever had returned. When she tottered off the stage at long last, too tired and sore to bother being brave, she collapsed with a sigh of relief in Ivy's arms.

"I must say, I'm shocked at your appearance," Ivy told her when Mattie was at last resting in a warm bed with clean sheets. "If this is what the Pony Express does to you, it is no wonder I had such misgivings."

"I just caught a bit of a chill," Mattie said weakly.

Ivy tucked warm bricks underneath the sheet to warm Mattie's feet. "I have a notion there's more to the story. But we'll talk later. We'll get you better first. You need rest, hot food, and quiet."

Ivy was as good as her word. She asked no questions. She brought Mattie broth and tea and crackers and warm quilts. She read to her and she let her sleep.

Mattie felt herself grow stronger under her sister's care. She felt bruised from her experiences. Her body was sore, but her heart was worse.

She had long hours to think of Sam. The fury she'd felt for him faded, and she only felt the love. But it was like a hard, cold stone inside her. It hurt, and she was never free of it, except in sleep. So she went on sleeping.

Then Ivy arrived in her room one day with a purposeful tread different from her usual soft step. She sat down on the bed, jouncing the mattress.

"You can't sleep your life away," she said.

Mattie peeked sleepily at her from underneath the quilt. "I'm sick," she said, aggrieved.

"You're better," Ivy said. "I can see that. And I'm tired of running up and down the stairs fetching for you."

"Oh, Ivy," Mattie said, struggling to sit up. "I am sorry. I will get up."

Gently, Ivy pushed her down again. "Now, hush. I don't mind taking care of you, Mattie. That's not the point. But if you keep abed like this, you'll just have a harder time once you do get up. I want you to come downstairs and sit in the parlor. We'll keep you well wrapped."

"The parlor?" Mattie's heart sank. She wouldn't mind fetching food for herself and bringing it upstairs. But she didn't want to sit in the parlor, where she'd have to be sociable.

"You'll get more air and light there, and you need to use your legs," Ivy said, smoothing the quilt with a determined hand.

"All right," Mattie said grudgingly. She knew better than to argue with Ivy.

"Now, before we go down, I want you to tell me what's wrong," Ivy said. Her warm brown eyes softened. "I've never seen you this way, Mattie. I'm worried. It's not just your body that's hurting, is it?"

Mattie wanted to tell her everything. She wanted to tell Ivy about Sam, how she loved him, how stubborn he was, how she'd hurt him, how he'd deserved it. Ivy gave wise and gentle counsel.

But for the first time in her life, Mattie couldn't confide in her sister. These feelings were different. They were too tender to expose. They were too private, too precious, and she was feeling too weak to talk about them. Maybe later, after she'd quit the Express, she'd be able to tell Ivy everything. But not yet.

"It was harder than I thought it would be," she said finally. "I faced death, Ivy, and I guess I found out I wasn't as brave as I always congratulated myself on being."

Ivy patted her leg. "Well, that's natural. We never know how brave we'll be when faced with something awful. Sometimes we surprise ourselves with our bravery, and sometimes it's the other way 'round."

"I suppose," Mattie said dryly. "But I'd rather have surprised myself pleasantly."

Ivy laughed. "I think you're being too hard on yourself, Mattie. From the little you have told me, I think you were very brave. You swam that river even though you knew how dangerous it was. But you'll have to tell me the whole story. As a matter of fact, it's time you did. I'm going to write about you, remember?"

Ivy gave a weak smile, and suddenly Mattie noted how tired and worn her sister looked. "Is something wrong, Ivy? Tell me."

Ivy pressed her lips together and looked down at her clasped hands. "It's Justus. He's written to his father that he won't be returning to Georgia. Not only that, he's supporting Abraham Lincoln in the coming election. I'm afraid he's cut himself off from his family forever."

"I'm sorry to hear it," Mattie said. "But Justus is used to taking the unpopular position."

"And it costs him," Ivy said. "Why do you think he works so hard? Why do you think he chooses the cases that he does? It's as though he's making up for the sins of the whole world, just because of the way he was raised—the things he saw . . . the things his family profited by. For some men, injustice burns like a brand, and it never heals. And if war should come . . ." Ivy shuddered.

"Oh, there won't be a war, Ivy," Mattie assured her. "People are smarter than that. There's so much at risk: young men's lives and the country's future. Why would folks want to rip the Union apart?"

Ivy's eyes were sad. "Oh, Mattie. When it comes to war, people aren't smart. And they're not reasonable, either." She roused herself, patting Mattie's hand. "But we should speak of happier things. Come along downstairs, love. I want to hear all about your adventures. It's quiet now. We can begin."

Wrapped in a quilt, Mattie sat on the parlor sofa and talked. She talked for three days while Ivy listened and laughed and gasped and scribbled notes by her side. She prodded Mattie with questions, her expression keen.

But all the while Mattie spoke to her sister of raging rivers and black nights, all the while she described riding underneath a purple sky and a fingernail moon, she was thinking of Sam.

If she wanted him, shouldn't she do her very best to get him? And wouldn't the best way be by becoming a girl?

Maybe she should get herself that white dress. And a parasol. Definitely a parasol. She'd cover her shorn hair with the most cunning hat she could find.

She could pout at him or toss her head and pretend to be angry. Mattie had always thought feminine wiles were mighty silly, but she was crammed into a boardinghouse with other single young women in a mining town, and she'd seen how they worked. She'd thought that men were incredibly stupid to fall for them, but fall for them they did, and they didn't even seem to mind. They seemed to enjoy the game, silly as it was.

She was sure that it was only pride that made Sam so prickly. He couldn't bear being shown up by a girl. Maybe he needed to be shown how girlish she could be.

Mattie pictured herself ducking under a parasol and batting her stubby eyelashes. She tried to picture Sam being impressed, but the picture didn't fit.

When she got right down to the nub of it, it just wasn't her. Mattie sighed.

"Tired, dear?" Ivy asked. She dropped her pad. "We can stop."

"I am, a bit," Mattie said.

"Perhaps some tea."

"That would be lovely."

Ivy rose and rustled off. She was so graceful, Mattie thought enviously. But Mattie couldn't win Sam that way. The trouble was, once she started being graceful, she'd have to keep on doing it, and it would be too much of a strain.

She'd just have to jog on as Mattie Nesbitt, dressed in boots and pants. She'd have to risk losing him to get him.

When Ivy returned with the tea, Mattie took a cup and sipped it.

"What is it?" Ivy said. "You're going to tell me something, aren't you?"

"I think it's time I went back," Mattie said.

Ivy sighed. "I was afraid of that."

Mattie covered her sister's hand with her own. "It's time. And I only have a few runs left. I want to finish out the two months, Ivy."

"I know. But you've barely been off the sofa—"

"I'll start walking today. By Friday I'll be ready."

Once she had determined to go, Mattie bent her will toward it. She walked about, getting her muscles in shape. She ate big meals and got plenty of sleep. Ivy took her bundles of notes and disappeared into the pantry Annie had turned into a workroom for her. She would give Mattie the finished article on the day of her departure. Mattie herself would take the letter the first stage of its journey east to the literary journal Ivy wrote for.

On the morning she was to leave, Justus dropped by to say good-bye. They sat in the parlor, waiting for Ivy to put the finishing touches on her manuscript.

Mattie noticed the strain on Justus's face. To cheer him, she said softly, "Ivy told me of your troubles, Justus. I hope you don't mind."

He shook his head with a smile. "Not at all. You'll be my sister, too, one day."

"I just can't believe there'll be a war," Mattie said. "Or that your father won't forgive you, in time."

Justus's smile turned sad. "You and Ivy were lucky, Mattie. You grew up within a benevolent home. You never saw cruelty or injustice. I know your father took a misstep later in life, but before then, your life was good."

Mattie nodded, but she didn't quite see what Justus was getting at.

"I've seen things," he said painfully. "I wouldn't say it's made me bitter. At least, I pray not. But it has made me . . . wary."

Mattie saw the pain and struggle on Justus's face, and for the first time, she was truly touched by the sight. How shallow she'd been! She had never tried to understand him at all.

Justus had grown up, come to manhood, in a different world. She had never stopped to consider the forces that drove him to remake his life in California. He'd had his share of attacks from the community because he took on the cases of

Chinese and Indians and Africans in the Sierra. She had been bored by the law, bored by his cases, and never bothered to listen. She had been too busy planning her next run or wishing to be out underneath the wide blue sky.

Maybe it was time she did listen. Justus was right. She'd grown up with grace and rationality. She didn't know about brutality or cruelty. Maybe she needed to know in order to understand the world. In order to understand Sam. She needed to look under the surface and find the man.

"Justus, how did you come to know Sam Brand's family?" she asked tentatively.

Justus roused himself, seemingly grateful for the change of topic.

"I don't know them well," he admitted. "But what I know, I admire. I helped his father devise a will. If he dies, he wants his property to be left to his wife. He thought there might be problems because she's Indian. The Brands have good cause to distrust the white man's laws."

"Why is that?" Mattie asked, alert.

He leaned forward on his knees. "When Sam was eight years old or thereabouts, his father left on an extended trip, hunting for beaver pelts. He left Sam and his mother in their cabin up on the Feather

River. And he asked Sam's mother's sister and her husband to stay with them for protection. A couple of prospectors found the cabin, violated Sam's aunt, and killed his uncle in front of him. They nearly killed his mother, too, but instead they spared her and took Sam. They forced him to work for them, prospecting upriver. Sam's mother couldn't get him back. Under California law, Indian children can be taken as servants. Sam was mistreated, forced to work for brutal men."

"I didn't know that," Mattie said. Her tongue felt thick suddenly. She felt rooted in her chair like a stump.

"Slavery isn't just in the South," Justus said bitterly. "I hear there's a regular slave market for Indian children down in Santa Fe."

"What happened to Sam?" she whispered.

"His mother had no recourse. As an Indian, she couldn't speak against the men in court. They kept Sam at hard labor for almost a year before his father, who had been ill, made his way home. He got Sam back by calling on some friends and taking him by force. Mattie, are you all right? You look awfully pale suddenly."

She swallowed. "I'm fine."

Ivy hurried into the room, carrying an envelope.

"It's finished at last, thank goodness. My editor is holding up the issue, waiting for this, Mattie." She thrust it into her hands.

"I'll be taking it myself tomorrow," Mattie replied woodenly.

Ivy and Justus kissed Mattie, telling her to be careful. She waved her good-byes and walked to Willie Joe's, where he'd saved space for her on his wagon.

She felt emptied out. She felt criminally stupid. She felt inexcusably naive.

She had been full of her own ideas. Puffed up with her own experience. She had belittled his fears, right to his face. She had mocked his concerns, and she had dishonored him. Arrogance had gone hand in hand with her love. She had thought she knew Sam Jackson Brand down to the bottom.

But she'd never really known him at all.

CHAPTER TWENTY-ONE
A KNIFE IN THE HEART

"Looks like tomorrow'll be your last ride, Matt," Alfie told her when she got to Friday's Station. "The regular rider's leg is healed, and I promised him he could have his job back. Maybe I could put a word in for you further down the line—"

"Thanks, Alfie," Mattie said. "I think it's time I went home."

"Just as well," Alfie said, meditatively lighting his pipe. "Seems there's Indian trouble along the Fort Churchill route. You just might get an arrow through you if you stay."

"Paiutes?" Mattie asked.

"They're riled up about something or other," Alfie said, waving his pipe. "Seems they're awful touchy about their womenfolk. Some fellows imprisoned them in a cave, just having a bit of fun, and I hear the savages were not impressed, no sir." He chortled, then choked on his pipe smoke.

"Sounds like a heap of trouble for a couple of squaws, to me."

Mattie turned away. She'd liked Alfie fine at one time. Now she felt relieved to be leaving his station.

"Sounds like white men would feel the same," she said.

"They don't feel about their women like we do, sonny," Alfie said. "Besides, those dirty Paiutes don't need a reason to go on the warpath. They've bedeviled their share of riders, let me tell you."

"Maybe because we're riding across their land," Mattie said. Alfie gave her a disbelieving look, and she turned to pour herself some coffee. No use getting in an argument.

So she didn't say what she wanted to say, what she'd been pondering. That the Paiutes weren't stupid. They knew that mail service meant more people, and more people meant cities and laws and treaties. And the telegraph would come, bringing more people and maybe a transcontinental railroad one day. And then there would be few Paiutes left to harass those crossing their lands.

The next morning she had a few hours before Sam was due on his run. To avoid talking to Alfie, she settled in her bunk with Ivy's story. She turned the pages hungrily, eager to see her experiences through Ivy's eyes.

She wasn't disappointed. In her crisp, exciting prose, Ivy had turned Mattie's story into a thrilling adventure. The rescue on the river was written with such urgency that Mattie could almost taste her terror again.

There was one problem. Ivy had focused on the friendship between her and Sam. Even though Mattie hadn't dwelled on it, Ivy must have sensed the connection between them. She included the story of the peddler, and she included Sam's parentage. Mattie hadn't told Ivy that Sam was half-Indian. Justus must have done it innocently, not realizing it wasn't common knowledge.

Ivy had written movingly of their friendship. For her, it was a tale of two of society's outsiders finding strength in themselves as well as each other.

But Mattie knew everyone would know who Sam was. The story of their encounter with the peddler had been passed down the line. Everyone knew it was Matt who had stepped up to that gun. Everyone knew that it was Sam who had rescued her from the river.

And now, not only would they know her secret, they would know Sam's. For him the story wouldn't be a pleasant tale, spun out for thrills and gentle lessons about brotherhood and courage. For Sam it would be a knife in his heart.

"You got that letter for me?" Alfie asked. "I'm packing up the mail to add to the *mochila*. I want to slip one in myself, to my wife back east. I write her once a year like clockwork."

Mattie had no choice. She sealed the envelope and handed it reluctantly to Alfie. Now the letter was registered with the Pony Express.

Nervously, Mattie gathered her gear. Her horse was tethered outside. She waited on the porch, her feet tapping a nervous tattoo on the boards. It reminded her of her very first ride. It felt like years ago that she'd seen Sam Brand leaping off his horse and throwing the mail to her.

"I see some dust," Alfie remarked. "That's him, all right. We're in business!"

Mattie mounted. She'd almost forgotten how quickly the rider came up once you spotted him. He went from a black speck on the horizon to a horse and rider, rising and falling against the sky. And then you could just pick up the flutter of hooves, and shading your eyes, you saw a familiar shape of a hat, the particular seat of the rider. Then, in a moment, he was on you, and you were moving, securing the mail and galloping for all you were worth.

Today she would break a rule. She would take a moment, the barest whisper of a moment, to say a word to Sam.

She'd risked her life for the Pony Express. Surely they could grant her a word.

Sam pounded up. The mail was transferred from his hand to hers and secured behind her saddle. He was turning away when she put a hand on his shoulder.

"Sam—"

He looked back, startled.

"Matt, get moving!" Alfie bellowed.

She looked straight into his face. "I was wrong," she said.

"If you don't get that horse going, I will!" Alfie roared, running toward her with his arms flailing.

She only saw confusion in Sam's eyes. There was no time, no way to say more. Disappointed, anguished, Mattie rode off.

CHAPTER TWENTY-TWO
THE LAST RIDE

Mattie thundered down the dusty road. The journey to her first swing station at Genoa was her favorite part of the trip. It ran through lovely country ringed with mountains, and the road was good.

But today she didn't scan the hills or breathe in the fresh dry air. She felt as though there were a stick of dynamite in her *mochila*. It was Ivy's story.

She couldn't let it be published. She couldn't bear the thought of Sam reading it or hearing about it. And he would. Ivy was a popular author, and her work was the subject of much discussion in the Sierra.

She could damage Ivy's reputation if it never reached her editor. The man was holding the presses, waiting for it! And Ivy herself would be heartbroken. She would forgive Mattie, but she had been excited about the story. She felt it would truly strike a blow for western womenfolk. Look what we are doing out here! it would say. Look at what we're capable of!

So far, despite Indian attacks and severe weather, the Pony Express had never failed to deliver each letter entrusted to its care. The mail had always gotten through. Could she be the first to break that trust?

Mattie galloped into Genoa. The town lay cradled against a slope at the base of the mountains. She had enjoyed her brief glimpse of the Carson Valley before her. She could trace the course of the river with her eyes and be refreshed by the thought of its coolness.

Today she didn't notice the view. She swung onto the fresh mount at the station and went on riding. Carson City lay ahead.

The thundering of hooves beat a message to her brain. She couldn't let the story be published. She couldn't let the envelope pass from her hands to another's.

Mattie pulled back on the reins. She slowed her horse, then brought him to a halt. She reached behind her for the leather pouch. Unbuckling it, she rooted inside.

She held Ivy's letter up. Ivy would just have to forgive her. The Pony Express would just have to forgive her. She tucked the envelope into her shirt. Then she spurred her horse on.

Funny how things happened sometimes. She didn't know if she and Sam would be together. But she was willing to break an oath to spare his feelings.

At first everything looked normal ahead. The Carson City station sat, isolated and peaceful. But Mattie had only galloped a few yards when a warning ticked in the back of her brain. Something was amiss.

There was no horse standing out front.

Even as she continued to gallop, Mattie let out a groan. Del. He was trying to rile her. She just hoped the pony was behind the station, already saddled. This would take minutes off her time.

But as she galloped up and tethered her horse to the rail, disquiet nudged aside exasperation. Surely Del should have heard her arrive. Surely he wouldn't carry a joke this far.

But the place seemed eerily deserted. Yelling his name, she grabbed the *mochila* and hurried toward the station. Her boots sounded a hollow beat as she started for the door.

"Hello?" she called.

No answer.

Now Mattie worried. The area had its share of bandits. They could be lying in wait inside.

She eased her revolver from her belt and held it ready, then opened the door slowly.

The station was deserted. With a sigh, Mattie tucked her revolver back into her belt. She'd go out back, where the ponies were kept, and bring one around. And she'd have to tend to the one she'd just ridden from Genoa. How could Del have been so careless?

She clucked in exasperation, started to turn, and then she saw it. A dark stain on the floor. She followed it with her eyes and saw it was coming from behind the high counter at the rear.

Holding her breath, moving as though in a dream, Mattie walked forward and looked behind the counter.

Del was lying on the floor, scalped. And very dead.

She gasped and her hand flew out, disturbing the papers on the counter. They fluttered down and covered Del's large body like a shroud.

She backed away, swallowing, swallowing, trying to tamp down her terror. She had to get out of there, get to the next station. Or should she ride to town and warn them?

The possibilities buzzed in her head like angry

bees, making it impossible to think. Mattie kept backing up, trying to think, to plan.

She bumped into something. Not a wall. A person. Someone who'd entered so silently she hadn't been able to discern a whisper of sound.

She turned and met a bronzed chest. She looked up into the face of a powerfully built Paiute.

Behind him were six others. And one of them closed the door.

CHAPTER TWENTY-THREE
A WARRIOR FIT FOR THE SKY

Mattie willed herself not to flinch. She knew that Indians admired courage.

She held up her hands in a peaceful gesture. The brave in front of her reached out and lifted her revolver from her belt. So now she was unarmed except for her knife. But the Indian had seen that, too, in the sheath hanging from her belt. He took it as well and handed it to another, who hefted it approvingly.

The Paiutes stared at her with expressions she could not read. She felt sweat break out, seemingly from every pore. There was one thing she must prevent. She must not let them find out she was a woman. In retaliation, she was sure they would do unspeakable things to her. Alfie had not said what the white men had done to the Indian women. But she could guess.

The tall brave spoke to the others, and one responded. They appeared to be commenting on her appearance, and she didn't think they were impressed.

The tall brave poked her in the chest. He hit softness, and surprise flared in his eyes.

She balled her hands into fists as he poked her again. He laughed and said something to the others.

The Indian who held her knife came forward. He reached out with the gleaming blade. Mattie had time for a spurt of pure terror before he flicked her hat off her head with the knife's point.

They laughed again.

Cold fear raced through Mattie's veins. She locked her knees so that her legs wouldn't shake. The tall brave reached out and ran a hand over her short hair. She didn't move a muscle.

"Not very pretty," he said.

She indicated his long hair with a nod. "Not like yours. Pretty."

After a startled moment, they laughed. But Mattie did not delude herself that she was charming them. She knew what danger she was in. This was war.

The brave grabbed her by the arm and roughly pulled her toward the doorway. Was she to be a hostage, then? Mattie quailed. She knew terrible things could happen to hostages. But each tribe was different. Some treated them, if not kindly, at least respectfully, taking them for money or concessions they could bring. She didn't know very much about the Paiutes, and she cursed her ignorance.

They started for the door, pushing Mattie before them. But then a miracle appeared.

Sam stood in the doorway. Dusty, grimy, weaponless. He held up his hands, then made a motion with them. The brave answered him with a gesture of his own.

Then Sam spoke a few words in a language Mattie assumed was Paiute, for the brave responded.

The grip on her arm didn't lessen. But the Indians spoke to Sam. He now made a wide gesture and pointed upward. Mattie waited, hardly daring to take a breath, while the conversation went on. It was impossible to tell what Sam was saying and impossible to gauge the Indians' reaction.

But suddenly the brave dropped her arm. As silently as they had appeared, the Indians left. They walked out in a dignified fashion, not a trace of hurry or agitation in their step. They even shut the door on the way out.

Sam quickly crossed to her side. "Are you all right? Did they hurt you?"

"I'm all right," she said. "But Del isn't. He's dead, Sam. Behind the counter."

Sam walked over and looked. He flinched. "Poor

Del. He'll be a hero now, just for getting scalped. Pity he won't be here to enjoy it."

"What did you say to them?" Mattie asked curiously. She leaned down to pick up her hat.

"That you were a great warrior and deserved their respect," Sam replied. "That you were a warrior fit for the sky."

"And that made them go away?"

"I also told them I saw three owls on the roof as I came up," Sam said. "Owls are a bad omen to the Paiute. But mostly I think I just gave them a reason to go. They'd done the work they'd come to do."

Suddenly he stiffened. "Let's go."

"Why?" Mattie said as he pulled her. But then she could smell it, too—smoke. And she heard the crackling of flames.

Sam had her by the arm and grabbed the *mochila* with the other hand. Mattie worried that the door would be blocked somehow, but Sam opened it without trouble. They ran out and saw that the roof was on fire.

"Del!" Mattie exclaimed. "We have to get him, Sam! We can't . . . leave him like that."

Sam's eyes were bleak. "It's too late, Mattie."

"It can't be," she said, tears springing to her eyes. She started toward the station.

Sam held her back, imprisoning her in his arms. "No, Mattie! Look!"

Half of the roof caved in. Sparks flew toward them, carried by the wind. Mattie closed her eyes and said a swift prayer for Del.

They stood watching as the roof collapsed. The fire was a blast of heat against their faces.

Mattie leaned against Sam for a moment, grateful for his support. Her eyes smarted from the smoke, and tears ran down her cheeks. Only yesterday, she would have given anything to feel his arms around her again. But not like this.

From out back, they heard the high whinny of a pony.

"The horses!" Mattie cried. She ran, choking from the smoke, around the side of the station. She was just in time to see the Paiutes riding away, taking the station's horses with them.

Then there was only blowing smoke and the sound of the flames.

CHAPTER TWENTY-FOUR
BELONGING

"Looks like we're in for a hike," Sam said. "Let's get away from this smoke."

He led her yards away to the shade of a tree. They stood for a moment and watched the station burn.

"We should meet someone on the road," he said. "They'll see the smoke and come running."

Mattie wiped at her wet cheeks. "Poor Del. You'll have to tell Alfie."

Sam nodded. "I have a feeling he'll have more than his share of grief." He sighed. "Come on. We'd better start walking."

They returned to the front of the station, and Mattie retrieved her hat from where it had fallen. As she bent over, Ivy's letter fell out of her shirt.

"What's that?" Sam asked curiously. "Is that part of the mail?"

"Sort of," Mattie said, shoving it in her pocket. "It's a story Ivy wrote. She's sending it back east."

Sam frowned as they began to walk. "I thought you said your sister was a seamstress."

A flush of guilt reddened Mattie's face. She had told so many lies! "She's Audacia El Dorado," she admitted, using Ivy's pseudonym.

Sam whistled. "And that's one of her stories? So why isn't it in the *mochila*?"

"Because I was going to destroy it," Mattie said hesitantly. "It's about me—and you. It doesn't use our names, but anybody who knows us would know it was us."

Sam raised an eyebrow. "Did she say something about you that you didn't like? And won't she be riled that you're not sending it?"

Mattie pressed her lips together. "She said you were half-Indian. She didn't know it was a secret, Sam. I just can't let it happen. Because you were right," she blurted. "I know that now. I was stupid to think I knew better than you how white folks really feel about Indians. I didn't want you to lose your job on account of me."

To her surprise, Sam laughed. "Well, it's too late now, Matt. I already *lost* my job. I was sitting eating some of Alfie's awful stew when I heard about the Paiutes. A group of men from over by Genoa came by—they were looking for a bunch of Indians to shoot. They said they heard there was going to be an attack on a station and they were going down the line, one after the other." Sam shrugged. "So I said I'd go alone."

"And they let you?"

"I think Alfie was afraid for Del and wanted to avoid his getting shot by mistake. And I reckon most of the men wanted to go back to their wives and families anyhow."

"But how did you convince them?" Mattie pressed.

Sam sighed. "I told Alfie *I* was an Indian. And it would be a better idea if I went, since I spoke some Paiute. I said it would be better to warn them instead of attack them. We don't want a full-scale Indian war. This is just how they start. One offense, then retaliation, then war."

Sam looked back at the burning building. "It's too late now. I expect there'll be more dead men before it's over."

"But how did you get fired?" Mattie asked. "I don't understand. You did a brave thing. And you were offering to save Alfie's son!"

Sam's face grew hard. "Alfie was perfectly happy for me to go. He just didn't want me to come back. Said that even if I disarmed the Paiutes, he couldn't trust me. 'Injuns are injuns,' he said. And with all the Paiute trouble, he'd never know if I was going to turn and be on their side."

"That's ridiculous!" Mattie sputtered. "Besides, you're not on anybody's *side*. You're just carrying the mail."

"One thing about human beings I've learned," Sam said. "And it's something I don't understand. Some of them like being mean."

She shivered. "I've sure fouled things up from start to finish. I've been a blockhead all around. I worried my sister and I hurt you, and now you've lost your job on my account."

"Mattie, we all do what we have to," Sam said. "Now who's bellyaching?"

A smile twitched at the corners of her mouth. "I'm not bellyaching."

Sam stopped. "Look at what happened today," he said gently. "You broke your oath as a rider for me. I revealed my secret for you. Shouldn't that tell us something?"

"Sure," she responded promptly. "We're both out of work."

Sam laughed. "The Pony Express won't last," he said. "They're losing money on it, day by day. It was just a scheme to promote the central route for the railroad, anyway. And the telegraph is coming.

We would have been out of a job within a year. Maybe less."

"So what will you do?" she asked. She held her breath. Would he go back up to the Columbia River to stay with his parents?

"Haven't had a chance to think about it," Sam said casually. "But I'm not leaving here."

She turned to him, hardly daring to hope. "You're not?"

"Who knows what mess you'll get into next?" he complained. But his green eyes twinkled.

"You mean you want to keep company with a *wallflower*?" she teased.

Sam groaned. "You heard me say that? I was just embarrassed, Mattie. I thought you were pretty." He eyed her speculatively. "But now that I've been around you some, I changed my mind."

Her heart fell. "You did? It's my hair, isn't it. Or the pants."

"I think you're beautiful," he said simply.

He drew her to him in a fierce kiss that knocked out breath and talk, fears and questions. He held her tightly against him, keeping his hand on the back of her head as though he meant to have her as close to him as possible.

"For the first time in my life, I feel like I belong

somewhere," he said when he released her at last. "I'll just have to find a way to be able to stay around these parts."

"I have a freight business back in Last Chance," Mattie said, breathless. "I could use a partner. And I hear you have some experience hauling mail."

Sam grinned. "Then can I apply for the job?"

"You're hired," Mattie said.

He cupped her face in his hands. "I meant what I called you before. You are a warrior." His eyes gleamed. "Just remember who's boss."

"Of course I will," Mattie said sweetly.

"Wait a minute," he growled. "I meant *me*."

From a distance, they could hear the sound of hooves hitting dirt. Soon men would arrive, and there would be questions and anger, and a shipment of mail to deliver.

Mattie took the opportunity to steal one last swift kiss. "What do you say we take turns?" she suggested.

Experience the passion and desire of all the

BRIDES OF WILDCAT COUNTY

A sneak preview of
another romantic adventure

Dangerous: Savannah's Story

by Jude Watson

CHAPTER SIX
Two Arrivals and a Departure

Shelby surveyed the cramped quarters below with a shocked glance. It seemed impossible that eight girls would be crammed into the narrow space.

She only had a moment to pick a top bunk and stow her luggage before her roommates arrived. For the next hour, she introduced herself and heard life stories, took compliments and gave them back, and wondered how she could possibly remember everyone's names.

First came Ivy and Mattie who shared one bunk bed. Then came a nervous girl called Henrietta and her friend Fanny who had red hair and a ringing laugh. Fanny loudly pronounced herself way too plump for her bunk. The Angel Scarborough, whose name turned out to be Jenny, took the bottom bunk opposite Shelby's, and her friend Harriet Hawkes, as plain as Jenny was pretty, took the top.

There was barely room to turn around in the cabin once all of the girls were in it. Shelby wondered irritably why a few of them didn't return to the deck, but they were all too busy getting to know each other to budge. She tucked her legs underneath her and lay back on her bunk, staring at the ceiling and wishing they'd all go away.

A shrill voice interrupted her thoughts.

"I'm sorry, I must object. I was promised the very best accommodations, and—"

Mattie poked her head out the door. "Oh dear," she murmured. "Trouble."

"What is it?" Ivy asked.

"It's that Narcissa Pratt," Mattie whispered. She listened for a moment, then poked her head back in the cabin. "Apparently there's a . . . well, a woman of color on board, and Narcissa won't room with her."

"Miss Nesbitt?" Elijah's voice came to them clearly. "Could I speak with you a moment?"

Mattie slipped out of the cabin. In a moment, she was back, her face flushed but her manner composed. "I trust there would be no objection if the newest arrival slept in our cabin. We have plenty of room."

Her bright blue eyes dared one person in the jammed cabin to refuse. No one did. Shelby imagined that no one would even think of it.

Mattie nodded firmly. "All right, Mr. Bullock," she called.

Eli walked in with Opal Pollard. Shelby sat up, bumping her head on the bulkhead. Opal saw her and Shelby gave a quick negative shake of her head. Opal's gaze moved smoothly away.

"You can sleep here, Miss Pollard," Elijah said. "And I apologize for . . . any inconvenience." He turned to the rest of the girls. "We're getting under way, ladies. You might want to come up on deck."

Shelby slowly trailed after the girls. She was dying to confront Opal, but the girl eluded her, slipping off and joining a group of passengers in the stern.

Up on deck, the sailors were moving, untying lines and calling orders. Most of the girls crowded against the railing for a better view, but Shelby preferred to stay in the back. She didn't want to be visible from shore.

She forgot about Opal as she listened to the cries of the sailors, the orders given and repeated. Her heart lifted. The gulls wheeled overhead and the faint rays of the sun cast a feeble glow on the water. She couldn't wait for the ship to pull away from the dock.

Down the pier, a slight figure ran, waving one slender arm. Behind her, two sailors, each carrying a trunk, struggled to keep up. As the girl approached the ship, Shelby could just make out her words.

"Blast and damn! Don't you dare leave without me!"

The girl's bonnet flew off her head and flopped down her back, held by its ribbons around her neck. Curly dark hair spilled from its pins and streamed down her shoulders.

The sailor who had been bringing in the gangplank quickly lowered it again. The girl raised her skirts and hopped onto it with the ease of a dancer. She motioned at the two men behind her to hurry as she landed with a soft thump on the deck.

The men threw the trunks to the waiting sailors. The girl caught the sailors staring at her legs and hesitated a few moments before dropping her skirts. She smiled a decidedly wicked smile at the cutest sailor.

Definitely not a lady, Shelby thought.

Unconcerned at the stares of the passengers, the girl blew away a stray curl from her eye, untied her straggling bonnet, and smoothed the skirt of what Shelby felt was a rather garish striped silk dress. The ship blasted its horn and began to move out of the berth.

"Made it," she called to Shelby. "In the nick, I'd say."

She stepped up to the railing. The buildings of Manhattan began to recede as the ship sailed away into the harbor.

"Glad to see the blasted back of that city," she said pleasantly. She turned to Shelby and held out a hand. Startling emerald eyes twinkled in a delicate, pretty face. "I'm Eden."

"Savannah," Shelby answered. She felt the deck move beneath her feet as the clipper picked up speed. The sound of the horn made her jump.

Savannah, she thought, as she and Eden both turned without a word and looked out to the open sea. From now on she would train herself to call herself by that name, even in her head.

She liked the sound of it. It was a name for a girl who didn't simper at someone just because they wore pants. Who wasn't polite if it didn't suit. Who didn't waste her time with foolishness. A new name for a new life. She couldn't wait to begin it.